WAGON TRAIN TO INDEPENDENCE

AN OREGON TRAIL WESTERN ADVENTURE
THE HENDERSONS – BOOK 1

William Tresler

Contents

Chapter 1
The Hendersons

Clyde Henderson's blood froze in his veins. His greatest fear—in fact, the only fear that had come close to turning him back from his decision to brave the unknowns of the Oregon Trail—was coming true before his very eyes. It felt like a nightmare, but he knew it was all too real to be a dream.

The high-pitched, chaotic whooping and shrieking that filled his ears was more terrifying than anything he had ever heard. Though the galloping, ululating warriors were still high on the gentle slope above them, silhouetted against the hazy midmorning Kansas sky, their cries seemed to bore right inside Clyde's brain, unleashing a flood of almost paralyzing dread.

"Clyde! Get your rifle!" a voice yelled stridently, breaking the spell of the Pawnees bearing down on them.

Clyde hurriedly complied, rushing to the little overloaded prairie schooner and reaching for the steel and wood object he had picked up for the first time in his life only a couple of months prior. His hand was shaking. "Anna! Girls! In the wagon! Billy, you too, and no arguing!" he ordered his family sternly, feeling anything but in control. He felt responsible for the danger he had placed his family in, but there were no more choices to be made other than to fight for his life and the lives of his wife and children. "Matt, bring your rifle. We'll need all the firing power we can get."

"Yes, Pa," Matt replied obediently, but with a complete lack of enthusiasm.

"Pa, can't I stay outside too? I have my Baby Dragoon, and I can shoot better than Matt already. Mr. Morland even said so. Please?" Billy drew out the last word in a whine as he stuck his head out the front of the wagon.

"This is no time for theatrics, William Clyde Henderson! I need you to take care of your sisters!" Clyde thundered back at his son in the most authoritative voice he could muster. He could not let them see his fear. As long as they thought he was confident, he could protect them, and they would stay calm and think rationally.

Billy pulled a face and drew his head back into the wagon. Clyde joined his new neighbor and acquaintance, Landon Morland, and his only son, Brady, at the wagon ahead of the Hendersons', questioning for what felt like the hundredth time the wisdom of giving in to his youngest son's demands that he also have a firearm and learn to shoot. Billy's reasoning had seemed solid at the time: he wanted to be useful on the trail to the land of promise.

"You got any idea where George is?" Landon wanted to know, his left jaw muscle working furiously and his eyes darting back and forth between the approaching Pawnees and the halted straggle of wagons.

"No, can't say I do," Clyde replied, feeling a bit of worry joining in with the gnawing fear in his gut. Their attackers were coming closer, their whooping growing louder as they closed the distance.

Landon glanced up and down the wagon train once more, and then he appeared to decide about something. "Circle the wagons!" he cried out stridently, cupping his hands to his mouth. "Brady, run ahead and pull that first wagon around to the right."

"Sure thing, Pa," Brady replied, his eyes mirroring the steely determination in his father's. "Can Matt come help with the other wagons?" He shifted his gaze from his father's face to Clyde's, and the latter nodded.

Matt and Brady sped off, yelling, "Circle the wagons!" as they went. Frightened faces peered out at them as whips cracked, men shouted, and lowing, lumbering oxen leaned into their yokes and strained against the deadweight of the wagons. Breaking into a slow, shambling trot—too slow, it seemed—the lead oxen swung round and circled back toward the wagons at the rear of the train.

By that time, the rumble of thundering hooves shook the earth beneath Clyde's feet, and the war cries of the Pawnees seemed to drown out every other sound. They were quickly coming within firing distance, and Clyde could only just hear Landon commanding the young men to get the extra horses and cattle into the center of the hastily forming circle of wagons. "Don't any of ya shoot unless they fire at us first!" Landon commanded before he rushed to defend his own wagon against the oncoming attack.

Diving in behind the wooden box of the prairie schooner, he leveled the barrel of his rifle at the Indians. Clyde followed his example and took up a position behind his own wagon. The sight before him was fearsome, one he had never even expected in his wildest dreams. And he had several before embarking on what now seemed a not only foolhardy but doomed trip.

As the warriors drew near, their features stood out in spine-chilling detail. They painted their faces with red, black, and white paint. Some with stripes down their cheeks, some painted like highwaymen's masks, some in broad swathes across their faces.

Their heads were shaved, except for a strip of hair arching over the top of their scalps, accentuated with a bizarre brush of long, spiky hair that looked like it came from some kind of animal. Even that was colored red, black and white in varying patterns for each warrior. From each head, a single black and white eagle feather bobbed and shivered in the wind.

On their upper arms, bronze, silver or leather armbands glistened in the morning light. Some wore large brass medallions suspended from leather thongs around their necks, while others sported strings of colored beads. A broad necklace of what appeared to be dark brown fur, bristling with a row of long white claws—which Clyde could only assume had once belonged to a bear—festooned the bare, painted chest of the leader.

Clyde's mouth felt dry, and his heart beat painfully against his ribs. He watched the wild men split up as soon as they reached the trembling settlers and flow like water around each side of the circle of wagons. They were armed to the teeth, waving spears, long javelins, tomahawks, and wooden clubs in the air as they galloped round and round the terrified emigrants. Their horses' hooves kicked up choking clouds of dust as they sped by at bewildering speeds.

The riders kept whooping and hollering, and one even snatched a side of buffalo meat hanging on the outside of one wagon, but they did not try to shoot an arrow or toss a javelin.

Clyde heard a young child crying and swallowed hard. "I sure hope Anna is praying, God," he whispered, "'cause if I thought You'd listen to me, I would be makin' supplication right now like I've never made before."

The tension in the air was even thicker than the dust being kicked up by the hooves of the painted ponies. Clyde noticed what looked like blond locks of human hair swinging from the mane of a pale gray horse as it sped by. His palms felt sweaty as he readjusted his grip on the almost-new Mississippi rifle in his hands. He almost wished one of them would shoot an arrow, if only for the sake of breaking the mounting, leaden weight of suspense.

With every nerve on edge, he peered at the warriors still riding by and suddenly realized they were smiling. And not merely smiling, but grinning from ear to ear as if they were thoroughly enjoying the sight of the terrified white folks hunkering down, attempting to avoid a massacre. His mind reeled. Could he be seeing right?

Just then, the leader thundered past with his necklace of bear claws. He shouted something in his language, and uproarious laughter followed, as if in reply to Clyde's internal question. They passed the comment along to those who had not heard, and mirth followed it like a rippling stream, all along the line of men. Clyde watched the leader veer away from the group of wagons and ride off in a new direction, not the one they had come from, and give a sharp, high-pitched, two-note cry.

The moment they heard their leader's call, the rest of the men—Clyde estimated them at about thirty, although it had felt like there were two hundred at one point—rode off after the man with the bear claws, still laughing and whooping. He realized they all had some kind of loot hanging from their horses' withers and across their haunches. He distractedly wondered if it was possible that so many settlers had hung goods on the outsides of their wagons.

The whoops and shrieks faded away, together with the laughter, as the swells of the rolling prairie swallowed the group up. A breathless silence followed, broken only by the wailing of a baby and the plaintive cry of a young calf. Both were strangely comforting sounds to Clyde's ears. Even the birds were silent, as the whole prairie seemed to hold its breath, waiting to see if the laughing warriors would return to taunt their victims again.

The first man to stand up and speak was Landon. "We need to hold an emergency meeting," he stated flatly, as he stepped toward the center of the circle of wagons. Clyde stepped up to join him, brushing the dust and grass from his brown denim pants as he did so. His knees still felt weak, but he sensed his new acquaintance was taking up a vacant position of authority in the group. He felt compelled to support such initiative, especially from the man who had, from what he could tell, been the reason for their coming through the ordeal unscathed.

Slowly, with fearful glances in all directions, the cowering pioneers emerged from their hiding places and gathered in a whispering, muttering huddle around Landon and Clyde. The latter's family gathered around him, except for Matt, who stood over by the Morlands, unconsciously mimicking Brady's confident stance but proving all the same that he was a city boy through and through.

"Has anyone seen George Barker?" Landon asked.

"Can't say we have," a swarthy woman replied as she peered from beneath her narrow-brimmed, faded, black felt hat.

"Last I saw, he led that flashy English thoroughbred of his back the way we came at a spanking run," a brash voice cut in.

Clyde turned to see a young man he knew only as Connor, chewing on a wad of tobacco with his thumbs hooked in his gun belt. He appeared to be trying very hard to make up for his New England accent and pale, city-bred skin.

They made a quick search of the wagons at Landon's command, but the searchers came up empty. Their leader had deserted them. Somehow, Clyde felt that was a good thing. It had made room for a genuine leader to stand up. He decided then and there to learn everything he could from Landon Morland.

"Right, folks, this is how the land lies," Landon went on, planting one foot on the ant heap that stood beside him. "The way I see it, we ain't got a man here knows the prairie better than me. I'd be happy t' step back if one of y'all can come forward and prove that ya do. Most important thing is that the feller in charge knows what he's about, if we don't want t' end up donatin' all our scalps."

He waited, scanning the bleak faces before him. Nobody made a sound. He grunted, nodding as he did so and adjusting his position to a more balanced and comfortable one.

"Well, then, I reckon that leaves me. First things first, we'll be needin' us some rules. Number one, every man gets a half a night of standing guard, and we'll rotate. Any man who falls asleep on watch will spend the next day walkin' beside his horse, not ridin' him. Number two, we will fire rifles in the mornin', five o'clock sharp, t' get us all up out o' bed, and at eight o'clock nighttime. That's the latest any of y'all can hit the sack. We need us enough sleep. Tired heads can't think straight, and a man needs t' think straight if he wants t' stay alive on the prairie."

Clyde listened to Landon's voice rattle off the rest of the rules he had already heard him bemoan the lack of under the previous leader's guidance. He could never have expected the anxiety that a lack of guidelines could produce in him, but now, hearing Landon lay down the law in no uncertain terms, he knew they would all be okay.

His mind wandered back to the happenings that had resulted in his family's journey out into the wild prairie. Back in Philadelphia, after the Great Panic had ended, the building trade had slowly been picking up, but Clyde had dreaded each day's work.

Nobody wanted beautiful structures or bothered about pleasing colors or grains of wood. All they wanted was the plainest, cheapest materials. It was as if the entire city was determined to stay on the bread line, eking out a drab existence and turning over every last penny in a pessimistic effort to avoid lack.

It felt, to Clyde, that the very act ushered in a lack far greater than money. He had never placed much store in that, anyway. The driving force behind all he did was to leave a legacy, not only for his children but for all who were surrounded by his work. He wanted to bring beauty and excellence to the simplest things. Without it, his life didn't feel worth living.

Anna had noticed his lackluster mood that had lingered for months, and eventually she had remarked on it. He could hear her words in his head, even where he stood out there on the prairie, with Landon's voice droning on, drawing proverbial lines in the sand.

"Clyde, my love," Anna said gently as they bedded down for the night after a particularly drab and gray day of doing only the necessary. "It's clear to me you're not happy. You've not been happy for a long while, and the children and I can see it."

He raised himself up on one elbow to look down at his wife's dear face. "I've despaired of ever being happy again, Anna," he replied, the black emptiness of despair seeming to reach up from the depths of his soul and choke the smile from his face. "Something has to change, but I don't know what."

That very next morning he had found the single page of newspaper that changed everything, flung about by the wind in the street before their apartment. It had landed at his feet before the whirling dust-devil snatched it away again and slapped it against the fence behind him. In that instant, the words, "The Land Of Promise Is America's Manifest Destiny!" sprang out at him from the crumpled paper and burned themselves into his brain.

"Manifest destiny," he whispered to himself, as he quickly turned and retrieved the ragged scrap of old news from the wooden fence behind him. The words seemed to open up a glimpse of what felt like light at the end of an endless tunnel, the faint hope there might be a future beyond the drab, dreary existence he had been living.

He scanned through the article while he walked down the street on his way to work. The paper was two years old, a January 1844 issue of The Inquirer. The provocative headline realized its full glory in the glowing and vision-inducing words that followed.

"It is our Manifest Destiny, as a nation, to take hold of this promised land and be the good stewards she needs us to be, in order that she may become a part of this magnificent nation. With this goal in mind, the government has offered, without any cost, a generous 320 acres to any man or woman and 640 acres to any married couple who undertakes the long, arduous, but excessively gainful journey across the Great American Desert and the Rocky Mountains to take ownership of their claim. The only other requirement is that each emigrant undertakes to work the land on their claim and produce crops for four years in order to claim the land as their very own."

Clyde almost bumped into a tram rumbling along the road as the words he read drew him further away from the reality of life around him. He could see the pine forests and hear the *rushing streams, smell the damp, fresh earth and feel the warmth of the sun on his skin. To say nothing of the acres and acres of open land, the slower pace of life, the appreciation for beauty that would give him a reason to not only build but create homes that expressed the joys and passions of those who lived in them.*

And yet, at the same time, it all seemed too good to be true. Along with the stories of unfettered abundance in the fairytale land beyond the Rockies came horrifying tales of marauding bands of wild plains dwellers, ferocious bear and wolf attacks, men falling to their deaths from spooked horses, children being killed by loaded rifles going off accidentally in the wagons, and long lists of illnesses—some deadly—with not a hospital in sight.

It was another three years before he reached the point where his frustrations exceeded his fears and he declared is intentions to his beloved wife, Anna. Her reply would stick with him for the rest of his life: "I've been waiting five years for you to say something, love. And you do not know how happy I am that the time has come."

Chapter 2
The Morlands

"Your boy's a real trooper," Landon remarked, cutting short Clyde's foray into the past.

"Matt?" Clyde replied, noticing the crowd of emigrants had dispersed and most were heading back to their wagons. "I worried he might be too soft for the wilds, but he's surprised me, I'll own."

"Looks like he's got calves' eyes for my Carrie, too," Landon added, nodding with a wink and a smirk toward his own family.

Matt stood with his hands behind his tall, straight back and his shoulders slightly drawn up. A barely discernible flush colored his cheeks as he spoke with a young woman who was clearly Landon's daughter. She had her father's direct gaze and her mother's fresh, golden-haired beauty.

Clyde chuckled to himself, feeling the tension of the last couple of hours begin to leave his jaw and neck muscles.

"I'd like t' thank you for keeping a level head through all this," Landon continued, his eyes becoming serious again. "Can't tell you what it means to have folks like you on a trip like this."

"We're grateful you took charge," Clyde assured him, then added, "Do you think they'll be back anytime soon?"

"Not too likely," Landon replied, to Clyde's great relief. "But I wouldn't bank on it. We'll have t' use the last few hours of daylight we have t' get ourselves further along the trail, soon as we're done noonin' here. We've got t' think of making decent time, too, apart from all the other shenanigans we'll be dealin' with."

"How did you know they wouldn't shoot?" Clyde prodded further, wanting to understand the ways of the wild land he had entered so naively.

"I didn't," Landon countered with a blank expression. "I took a bet on it. They were Pawnee. Kind of surprised me they attacked. They ain't usually the kind to do that. I figured they must be a renegade band. And they already had a ton of loot, and a few scalps, so they'd had them a plumb profitable raid already. Maybe the Mormons on the trail running alongside ours a ways north of here. I figured they might just be testin' our mettle. If we'd have shot first, things would have been a whole lot different, though, don't fool yerself."

"You really saved our lives, then," Clyde said soberly.

"I ain't the hero you think I am," Landon remarked, one side of his mouth twitching up in the ghost of a smile. "I was thinkin' of my own wife and kids before any of y'all, and that's no lie."

Clyde laughed, feeling the tension draining from his shoulders and down his back. "Well, long as I can get the leftovers of you rescuing them, I'm all in!"

"You know somethin', Clyde Henderson? You ain't half bad," Landon said approvingly. "I'd be happy t' have you as my second in charge if you'd be willin'."

Clyde hesitated. "I'm nothing but a carpenter looking to get out of the city," he said slowly, feeling unequal to the mantle of responsibility that the wagon train's new leader held out to him.

"Ain't what you know that counts," Landon shot back without missing a beat. "It's what you're willin' to learn, and you strike me as a feller who's happy to take good advice when it's to be had."

Clyde smiled sheepishly and shrugged. "Well, if that's all you're looking for, I suppose I'm your man," he replied.

"Why don't we have dinner together, your folks and mine, and we'll get to know each other a little better," Landon suggested. "I always like to know what a man's about when I'm fixin' t' work with him."

"Sounds like a grand idea," Clyde agreed, and the two men went over to their respective wagons to gather their families. They found the two women already working together to create a meal.

Anna looked up as they approached and gave her husband a brave smile. "Clyde, I hope it's okay. Louise suggested we join forces for dinner," she said, giving the woman beside her a grateful look.

"Well, that's very kind. Thank you, Louise. It's also just what your husband suggested," Clyde said, taking a seat on the couple's wagon wheel.

"Since we're neighbors, we may as well be good ones," Louise responded, giving Clyde a nod of acknowledgment.

He couldn't help thinking that, of all the people he had ever met, the Morlands had to be the most practical.

It was a simple dinner of pan bread and salty, almost tasteless bacon. Louise knew the local plants well and had dug up some wild onions and a strange tuber that looked almost like a potato, except it was very pale and rather bland in flavor. Louise referred to it as Indian breadroot and promised to help the Henderson children identify it so they could gather that, as well as the buffalo chips that fueled the fires every noon and evening.

"You say you're a carpenter," Landon said to Clyde between bites of food.

"I am," Clyde affirmed.

"You'll come in handy for fixin' wagons. They look sturdy, but the prairies are only the beginning. We'll be needin' a woodworker's skills, that's for sure."

"I'll help, too," ten-year-old Tessie piped up, her blue eyes bright and eager beneath her mass of dark, unruly curls.

"You know what to do with a hammer and nails, little miss?" Landon asked.

"She sure does, sir," Matt assured him, and Tessie nodded vigorously.

"I'd like t' see it," Landon replied with a smile. "But first, tell me what brought you folks out here?"

"I don't rightly know," Clyde admitted. "Other than wanting something to change. Life in the city isn't all it's made out to be."

"Well, life on the prairie ain't that glamorous either," a youthful voice piped up.

Clyde looked over to see one of the Morland sisters, a girl of about fifteen, creasing her pretty face into a resentful scowl. "I'd much rather be back in Columbia with my friends. I was planning to go to college this year, you know?"

"And how did you think Pa was goin' t' pay for your college with our ranch burned down, Helen?" Brady asked his sister with a frustrated frown, looking up from his tin plate that he was wiping clean with a piece of pan bread.

"Your ranch burned down?" Anna echoed, aghast. "That's terrible!"

"Yeah, could have been worse, though. We all of us came out alive by a miracle, plain and simple." Louise was gathering empty tin plates as she spoke.

"And I'm immeasurably grateful God saved your lives," Anna said brightly. "I'm not sure what we would have done without you here as part of our wagon train."

Louise paused and looked at her for a moment with a strange look on her face. Clyde wondered what was going through her mind, but she quickly broke off her gaze and went on collecting plates without comment.

Breaking the sudden lull in conversation, and apparently conscious all had eaten their fill, the train leader cast a practiced eye at the position of the sun and then stood up briskly. "All right, folks! Move 'em out!" he yelled.

Brady and Matt sprang to their feet and took up the call, echoing Landon's words. The settlers scrambled to cover fire pits with sand and stow away all the makings of the noon meal before hitching their oxen to their wagons again and cracking their whips to get the reticent beasts moving.

This time, Landon's wagon took the lead, oxen lowing and wood creaking as his outfit rumbled into motion. As soon as the line of oxen and wagons were firmly on the trail again, Clyde strode up to the front to walk alongside Landon.

"I'm curious to hear more of your story," he said. "How do you know the prairies so well?"

Landon grunted. "I ain't one for back stories, but since I asked your history, it's only fair you hear mine, too."

"Papa! Look!" the youngest of Landon's daughters ran up to him, pointing to a tree-lined rise in the not too far distance. "Wolves! Do you think they'll sing for us again tonight, Papa?"

"For your sake, I hope they do, Lucy," Landon said fondly. "Though I ain't sure the rest of the train will enjoy that little concert as much as you do, sunshine." He laughed, and the little girl, who Clyde guessed to be around twelve, skipped off to look for more buffalo chips and whatever prairie plants and berries could be consumed with the evening meal.

"I grew up poor," Landon picked up the conversation again as if there had been no interruption. "We lived near Scottville, Kentucky. Pa was a ranch foreman, Ma stayed at home and kept our cabin neat and clean and our bellies full. At fourteen, I became a ranch hand, workin' for the same ranch, but I swore I'd have my own one day. Pa and Ma helped by lettin' me stay on with only a little rent paid out of my cowboy wages while I saved the rest till I had enough to buy me a little packet of beeves."

"Humble beginnings," Clyde commented, trying to imagine a fourteen-year-old Landon roping steers and driving cattle across the plains.

"You could say that," Landon agreed. "When I could, I picked up odd jobs with other outfits, too, until I had enough to buy my own piece of land. Took me a coon's age, but it was worth it. All of fourteen years, if I'm honest, but I'd do it again in a heartbeat."

"And Louise?" Clyde prompted.

Landon's leathery features broke into a rare smile, and his piercing blue eyes stared almost worshipfully at his wife riding his horse on the opposite side of the plodding oxen. "She was the daughter of one rancher I rode for," he said, a faraway look on his face. "I knew she was mine the moment I saw her, but her pa would have none of it. He'd already promised her to one of his rancher buddies. Well, Louise was an apple didn't fall far from the tree. She upped and told her pa she wasn't one of his steers he could just palm off to the highest bidder, that she had her own mind and nobody was going to tell her how to use it."

He chuckled at the memory, and Clyde joined in. He could fully imagine her doing what Landon had described.

"I only heard this when she pitched up outside my little two-room cabin I'd just finished building that evening and asked me if I was going to propose marriage to her or not."

Clyde laughed again. "And what did you tell her?"

"I told her I would if she promised to say yes," Landon said dryly, as if reliving the moment. Then his eyes grew sad. "We worked so hard on that ranch, side by side. She was barely eighteen, but strong and stubborn as an ox. I was twenty-eight and ready to make my mark on the world. We sold off the land and moved out to Columbia a few years later, t' get away from the crowds. A bit like yourselves, I reckon."

"Oh, my family only moved with me because I asked them to, and they're the best a man could wish for," Clyde broke in.

At that moment, Billy, with his twelve-year-old freckled face and unruly auburn hair, came scampering up. "Pa! I saw a rattlesnake!" He turned his shining green eyes to look at Landon then. "I kept my arms still and stomped my feet in place, just like you said, Mr. Morland, and he took off like all hell was after him!"

"Watch your language, Billy," Clyde cautioned his son. "You know Ma doesn't like you talking like that."

"But, Pa, it's just us here, and I've heard Mr. Morland curse before," Billy pleaded, looking downcast that his father was more interested in his vernacular than his achievement.

"That's a mighty fine thing you did, young feller," Landon said, appearing not to have noticed the turn of the conversation. "I'd say you're a chip off the old block, here. You learn quick, just like your pa. I reckon you'll do yourself a favor to mind what he says. He's a fine man, the kind you won't find under every bush."

Billy looked a little taken aback. He glanced sideways at his father with an expression that almost made Clyde laugh. It was as if his son was seeing him with new eyes. Clyde silently thanked Landon for his subtle support and determined that if he was going to make a friend for life, Landon Morland would be it, as crusty and detached as he might seem to some. Matt called out to his brother from further down the line of wagons, and Billy scampered off again.

"So far, none of them regret coming out here with me," Clyde picked up their previous conversation. "It's all an adventure to them, a holiday, really. I'm hoping that'll last awhile still. At least until it's too late to turn back."

Landon chuckled. "They weathered that brief visit from our Pawnee friends pretty well, not like old George Barker, runnin' off with his thoroughbred," he quipped wryly.

Clyde grunted and gave his new friend a half-hearted smile. "I worry about him. We're already ten days out of Independence, and he has nothing but himself and his horse. Do you think he'll make it back?"

"The odds are stacked pretty high against him. Best chance he has is to turn right back around and join us again. I'll wager he won't." Landon paused, picking a shaft of long, green prairie grass as he strode along beside the wagon and began chewing the green end of it. The feathered flowers at the other end bobbed up and down as he stared into the hazy distance ahead of them. "We all have choices to make out here," he said gruffly. "And even makin' the right choices ain't a guarantee you won't get a visit from the elephant."

"The elephant?" Clyde asked, racking his brains to remember if he had heard that expression before and coming up with nothing.

"Bit of a nickname for death, I heard some other pioneers use," Landon explained, his eyes narrowing. He then quickly changed the subject, as if he was afraid that mentioning death by name might inadvertently invite it into their little group. "The Great American Desert's a few days from here. We won't be shootin' much out there. There's still buffalo, but they're far fewer than they used to be, as the story goes, and there ain't a tree in sight for miles. It'll be tough goin'. 'Specially with nothing t' keep us entertained."

"I'd better warn my brood," Clyde said grimly.

Landon nodded, then he pointed to the sun, already dipping low toward the horizon. "Time we found us a place to camp," he said pragmatically. A quick scan of the area revealed a slight hollow in the earth, with some trees screening it from the elements. Landon led his oxen toward it, and the rest followed obediently behind. Soon they had circled the wagons once more, and the glow of oil lamps and pit fires dotted the gray curtain of night falling.

"Pa, won't you play for us a bit?" a youthful voice said at Clyde's elbow as he sat by the fire, helping to roast a rabbit that Billy had shot while they were on the trail.

He looked up to see Nellie, his eldest daughter, holding out his fiddle and bow for him to take. The plaintive howl of a wolf somewhere in the night echoed into earshot just in that moment, and Clyde couldn't help but smile at the timing. "Any requests?" he asked as he tuned the strings.

"'Roll on Silvery Moon,'" Nellie chipped in eagerly before anyone could get a word out.

Clyde nodded and obliged, first warming up the bow on the quivering, responsive strings. The bubbling conversation around the glowing coals of the Hendersons and Morlands' shared pit fire faded away to occasional whispers as the haunting, melancholy strains of Nellie's requested song took flight among the sighing branches of the spruces surrounding their camp.

It was a perfect moment, and Clyde wished it could go on forever. He closed his eyes as he played, almost feeling his soul rise into the endless night sky. Promises came to his ear, whispered on the wind, but suddenly the mournful howl of the wolf sounded again, in near perfect harmony with the note he was playing. He knew there was heartache awaiting them somewhere along the trail. The question was not whether it would happen to them, but how they would come through it.

As the last vibrations of the final note of the song died away, a moment's breathless hush descended on the entire camp, until Billy's childish tones hacked through it like a wooden sword. "'Ol' Dan Tucker,' Pa! Play us 'Ol' Dan Tucker'!"

Clyde grinned. Leave it to Billy to brighten things up a bit. He played a fast, energetic line of double stops and then launched into the toe-tapping ditty with appropriate helpings of gusto and aplomb. Billy gave a whoop and grabbed Lucy Morland's hand, all but dragging her out into the middle of the circle. Laughing and yodeling, they sang the words between gasps for breath, boots stomping, and Lucy's skirts swirling.

> *Get out the way, get out the way*
> *Won't you get out the way, Ol' Dan Tucker*
> *You're too late to get your supper!*

Amid the rhythmic clapping on three beats out of four and the raucous singing, Brady jumped up and grabbed his sister Carrie's hand, and they joined Billy and Lucy in the middle of the circle.

May as well let them have a good time while they can, Clyde thought as he watched the revelry over the fingerboard of his fiddle. *Who knows what's waiting for us up ahead. We'll need all the joy we can get while it's to be had.*

Chapter 3
The Big Blue

Anna woke to the smell of rain hanging thickly in the air. Rising up, she peered between the thick canvas flaps at the front of the tent and found everything dripping wet. A gentle shower had silently soaked the camp overnight. Just then, the sound of bedraggled rooster crowing echoed through the damp air.

She pulled her head back inside to find Clyde struggling out from between their shared blankets. "I've got to sound off the waking up shot," he mumbled sleepily, blinking at his pocket watch in the gray morning light. He stumbled out and squelched his way to the front of the wagon. Moments later, she heard the rifle shot shatter the silence, and the sounds of waking travelers filled the air.

"Y'all better tar your wagon boxes before we leave. I reckon we should make it to the Big Blue crossing by late afternoon," Landon declared in a clear attempt at cheering up the miserable emigrants as they struggled to get fires going for their bacon to be fried over. "Independence Crossing, they call it."

"Independence Crossing?" Clyde repeated, as he paused in his shaking out of the tent canvas. "Seems like a real popular name along this trail. We started out at

Independence and now we're headed for Independence Rock."

"Funny they didn't call it the Independence Trail," Matt said thoughtfully, twisting a handful of hay grass that had stayed relatively dry under the wagon and holding it out for Anna to strike the flint to.

"They want us to keep rememberin' where we're headed, if you ask me," Louise interjected. "I heard there's a lot of folks branching off and heading for gold country or settling for claims somewhere along the way."

"Well, I suppose if we're really independent, we'll be free to make up our own minds about how far we go," Clyde added.

"I'd like to try my hand at mining for gold," Brady thought out loud while he helped his father grease an axle.

"No, you wouldn't," Landon assured him adamantly without elaborating on the reasons why his son's assumption about what he would like was wrong.

The young man smiled to himself and didn't respond.

By the time their hastily consumed breakfast was done and the families were packed and ready to hit the trail again, the sun had chased away the last of the straggly clouds and only a slight misty haze clung to the grasslands and copses of trees dotted about them. Anna walked and let the two youngest ride the family's horse, Buckaroo.

As she plodded along beside Buckaroo's nodding head, she could hear the disgruntled tones of Helen Morland carried back to her on the cool morning breeze.

"I'm goin' t' have blisters before we get to nooning, for sure. So much wet grass! My whole skirt is already wet just from walking through it. To think I could be nice and dry and warm in a college dormitory right now."

Nobody made any reply, mostly because they were busy enjoying the countryside unfolding around them. If they had thought the trail thus far had been beautiful, Anna felt like they had stepped through the mists of time and space and ended up in heaven. At the very least, the garden of Eden.

The grass was tall and thick and lush. So much so that the mules and oxen snatched mouthfuls of it as they lumbered by. Wildflowers of seemingly endless colors and shapes nodded and swayed to the rhythm of the dancing breeze, while the sun gently illuminated their glowing hues. Butterflies of varied sizes and patterns flitted about, along with dragonflies and the occasional buzzing of a beetle's clumsy flight accompanied the thud of hooves and creak of wagon wheels.

"Mama! It's so beautiful! You should paint it!" Tess enthused from Buckaroo's swaying back as she stared out, wide-eyed, over the vista around her.

The warmth of the sun beating on Anna's back drove away the chill of the wet morning, and she felt her spirits lift. "I certainly will, darling," Anna replied. "But I don't think I shall come close to replicating the masterpiece our dear Lord has created for us this morning."

"At least we'll be able to remember it better," Tess remarked, smiling. "You know, Mama, I know I didn't want to come out here when Papa said we'd be moving all the way to the other side of the world, but now I think it might have been a good idea after all."

"I can't wait till we get to bear country," Billy piped up, his eyes shining. "I'm going to kill me a bear and make a hat out of his head."

"Oh, Billy, no!" Tess protested, releasing Buckaroo's mane and pressing her hands firmly over her ears.

"But the Indians do it," Billy defended himself. "Brady told me. Maybe I'll make me a necklace of bear claws just like that Pawnee chief from yesterday."

"Hush, now, Billy," Anna chided gently, "you're upsetting your sister."

Billy drew up his lips in a snarl and made claws of his fingers while forming a deep-throated growl in Tess's ear where she sat in front of him. She gave a little shriek and jabbed an elbow into his ribs, at the same time kicking the heel of her boot into his shin and effectively turning his impression of a bear roar into a strangled yelp.

"Can't say I didn't warn you, son," Anna reminded him with a subdued laugh.

Billy scowled.

Anna turned her focus back to the unmitigated beauty around her as she left her children to sort out their brief altercation on their own. She drew a deep, appreciative breath. *So much beauty,* she thought. Yet *somehow, I know things will not always be this idyllic. I can only trust you will carry us through, dear Lord.*

The rest of the day was a blur of beautiful scenery, children catching butterflies, lush meadows and whispering winds caressing the tops of the trees scattered about the hillsides.

"Ooh! Look! That must be the river!" Billy called out when the midafternoon haze had thoroughly settled in and everyone was feeling a little more eager for their uncomfortable sleeping arrangements of wagon boxes and tents. Anna strained her eyes to see, but Billy was higher on Buckaroo's back. Then suddenly they topped the rise and the broad ribbon of tree-lined, foam-specked, winding blue water came into view.

Clyde came jogging back toward them. "Tess, Anna, hop in the wagon, let me up on ol' Buck," he said. "Billy, you can ride with me. Landon says this one's not deep. We'll make it through without swimming." He grabbed an ox's horn—the brindle one Billy had nicknamed Bacon, because he said the animal's coat reminded him of streaky bacon—and drew the draft animals to a weaving halt.

"It's deeper than the others, though," Billy said happily, shifting further back behind the saddle as his father helped Tess down and hoisted her up into the wagon. Anna clambered aboard beside her youngest daughter and peered round the canvas cover to see where Nellie was. The young girl had been picking flowers off to the side and now came bounding across the plain, one arm full of flowers, the other hiking up her skirts so she wouldn't trip and fall.

"I'll wade through, Pa," she said breathlessly as she reached them and Clyde swung up onto Buckaroo's back. "I hope I fall in. I could do with a bath right about now."

"Suit yourself, buttercup," Clyde replied with a grin. "The novelty'll wear off soon enough. May as well let you enjoy it while you can."

The lead wagon belonged to a young couple who had been way at the back the day before and therefore had the privilege of riding dust free up front of the train today. Anna watched their pair of mules balk at the water's edge. They sidestepped and snorted, tossing their heads. One lashed out with a kick, and the sound of splintering wood echoed up from the water.

Clyde and Landon immediately ran forward to help the couple with their stubborn draft animals, and eventually the two obstinate creatures relented under the persuasive end of a whip, lurching and leaping across the water as if they were convinced some vile monster was going to breach the waist-high depths and swallow them up whole.

"Close your ears, Tess," Anna said over the stream of curse words flowing from the mouth of the man who owned the obstreperous mules. "Nellie, won't you help Matt drive Ivy and the other milk cows over?" she called out to her older daughter as she jumped down from the wagon and went to grab the lead rope of their own two beasts of burden, Bacon and Butch. The patient oxen lumbered trustingly after her, their heads nodding as they strained against the weight of the wagon pressing the bows of the yoke into their necks.

Thank You, God, for bringing Landon across our path in Independence, she thought gratefully. *We might have been fooled into buying a pair of four-footed tearaways like those in the river now.* She remembered, with a shudder, how Landon had literally met them on the point of buying a pair of strong-looking mules, not dissimilar to the ones pulling the lead wagon so recklessly across the Big Blue.

She waded into the cool, rippling waters, clucking and calling to the animals she led. With hesitant but obedient strides, they stepped cautiously onto the uncertain ground, half hidden beneath the rushing waves. Anna felt a stone give way under her foot, and she almost toppled over into the river but kept her balance by hanging on to the oxen's lead rope.

With each step, the water rose higher along her skirts, the coolness more delicious on her hot, clammy skin than she had expected. She couldn't help thinking that Nellie's idea of falling in didn't sound all that bad, except she had two oxen following her. Ahead of her, the Morlands' wagon was already nearly rolling up onto the pebble covered shore on the opposite bank. Behind her, the next wagon team was gingerly testing the stability of the riverbed beneath their hooves.

Clyde came riding back with Billy clinging to his back like a leech. "Here, I'll take over," he said, holding out his hand for her to give him the lead rope.

"If I'm honest, I'm not sure how I'll get across if I don't have the rope to keep me steady," Anna admitted, loath to hand over her only support.

"Well, all right, I'll just ride alongside then, in case you need help," Clyde agreed, beaming down at her. "I knew I'd married right when I said my 'I do' to you," he added, a twinkle of admiration in his eye that made her blush.

"Oh, hush, you'll make me swoon," Anna joked with a giggle, and then took a bold step forward as she leaned more strongly on the lead rope. "Hup!" she cried out. "Hup, Bacon! Hup, Butch!"

Billy laughed out loud and joined in her chant as they splashed their way up out of the deep middle of the river and into the shallows again. Dripping and laughing, Anna felt the dependable firmness of the riverbank under her feet as she led the animals up out of the water and the wagon rolled on behind them. Everything safe and dry.

There was no chance of stopping. They had to make room for the wagons behind them, but now Clyde could take the rope from her and ride ahead of the oxen on Buckaroo. Anna stepped aside, trying to catch her breath as she waited for Matt and Nellie to make their way across the river with the milk cows.

They were already in the shallows, off to the side of the line of wagons, following each other across the rippling waters. Anna noticed a few wagons, the ones pulled by mules and George Barker's wagon—the only wagon pulled by two large chestnut Clydesdales—also fanning out to other parts of the river. Apparently, they were not willing to wait for the slow-moving oxen to cross before they took the plunge themselves.

She wondered again if George had made it to Independence with his horse and his scalp intact. The young man he had teamed up with had seemed perfectly happy to continue the journey on his own after George had failed to return, and he now had provisions for two people, a comfortable state to be in. Anna wondered how he would manage his rig on his own and suggested to Clyde that they offer assistance to him if he ever needed it.

Just then, she noticed Nellie waving to her as she stood laughing in the middle of the river. As Anna waved back with a smile, Nellie dramatically threw her hands up in the air and intentionally fell over on her back into the water. She came up clawing away the tendrils of wet hair clinging to her face while she sputtered and howled with laughter.

Papa's little flibbertigibbet, Anna thought fondly as she placed her hands on her hips in a mock scolding posture and shook her head even as she laughed. Then her eye caught Matt, carefully supporting a young calf that was trying to catch up to its mother across the deeper part of the river. *And to think they both came from my womb,* she mused, folding her arms across her chest and feeling the cool of her dripping dress against her legs.

There was something in the rawness of their new life that she loved even more than she had expected she would. Walking around in a wet dress would have earned her more than a few stares and whispers behind cupped hands. But out here, everyone understood what might make a woman want to keep wearing her sodden frock rather than exchanging it for a dry one.

It had not been an easy choice to follow Clyde on his quest for change. She had been comfortable enough in Philadelphia. Perhaps too comfortable. And Clyde had been absent in a way she could not remember him being before. She reflected on how he had almost disappeared into himself in the months before finally sharing his thoughts of following the Oregon Trail.

Now that they were out in the wilds, she felt like she had her husband back. And she realized a little more every day that she had not really fit in with the group mentality of the usual women of the city. Breathing the fresh air, discovering the fauna and flora through the eyes of her children, and seeing the wide expanse of the inky black heavens scattered with glittering stars each night had awakened something in her that had lain dormant for so long she hardly knew it was there.

Matt and Nellie trudged up the bank of the river, the milk cows and their calves ambling along before them, their coats dark from their soaking in the river. Satisfied that everyone in her care was safely across, Anna caught up to the wagon and found Tess sitting perched on the seat up front.

"Look, Ma," she grinned. "I'm driving!"

Anna smiled up at her while she walked alongside, and then the lead wagons slowed. Anna glanced at the position of the sun. It seemed to her about halfway down the western half of the sky, if she had to guess. Landon's prediction had been accurate.

By the time her skirts were dry, the sun had dipped almost to the horizon again, and suddenly she walked into what felt like a paradise. A rock shelf jutted out from a gentle slope and hung protectively over a shallow cave. Crystal clear water cascaded over the shelf, for what Anna estimated to be twice her husband's height, into a pool below.

From there, the water gurgled and splashed along a stony stream bed that wound its casual way down the hillside. All around, prairie grasses waved gently in the wind, while white ash and longleaf pines echoed the silent greeting. Birds twittered busily in the treetops, and a shy gazelle leaped away, disappearing into the undergrowth as the rumbling wagons approached.

Landon came riding along the train of wagons. "We'll camp here at Alcove Spring," he said. "We're lucky there ain't more pioneers takin' up space."

His words cheered Anna's heart. As soon as the wagons had circled, she took Clyde's hand. "Let's go to the spring," she suggested gently. "We can finish chores when we come back." Clyde nodded and called the children from their chores.

Standing behind the little waterfall, they gazed at the falling water and drank handfuls of it as it fell from the rock slab above. It was sweet and cold, reinforcing Anna's feeling of having stepped straight into heaven.

"Why don't you let us get supper ready while you make a picture of this lovely place with your paints," Clyde suggested suddenly.

"You really mean that?" Anna looked up at her husband, feeling as if her heart would burst.

"Well, you didn't bring those paints and canvasses along just to get them covered in trail dust, now did you?" he asked teasingly.

"You're right! I didn't!" Anna replied. She kissed him on the cheek and turned to leave. There were only a couple of hours of daylight left, and she did not want to waste them. "Children, be sure to play downstream so you don't muddy the water for drinking!" she called as she hurried back to the wagon.

That night, they slept well, despite the swarms of maddening mosquitoes that seemed bigger and more bloodthirsty than any Anna had ever seen. Even the howling of the wolves did nothing to strike fear into their hearts. But when the wake-up rifle shot echoed out over the camp, the emigrants woke to find their carefree sleep had not come without a price.

Chapter 4
Consequences

"The cows are gone!" The horrified cry rang out through the camp.

Nellie sat up, bumping her head against the wagon axle.

"Gone? Gone where?" another voice cried out.

"How do I know? To blazes, by the look of it!" came the agitated reply. "Where the hell is Norman?"

"Good question. It was his turn to watch. Now there's no sign of him or our cattle!"

"I'll wring his scrawny neck if I set eyes on him, I swear it on my mother's grave!"

The angry outbursts filled Nellie's ears as she scrambled out from under the wagon. She stood up and looked around. People were milling about, uncertain what to do.

"What's going on, Nellie?" Tess asked sleepily, lifting the wagon canvas and peeping out at the chaos.

Billy's drowsy, tousled head appeared beside his sister's, looking at her in bleary confusion.

"I don't know," Nellie responded, quickly returning her gaze to the direction of the angry voices. A huddle of men stood outside the far end of the circle of wagons, still waving their arms and talking rapidly and loudly. "You stay here," she added, quickly deciding. As she strode away toward the huddle of angry men, she noticed her father and Landon Morland headed in the same direction.

"What's going on, boys?" Landon asked in his deep, slow drawl that Nellie found so mesmerizing. She reached the group of disgruntled men soon after the two wagon train leaders did.

"Durned Norman's cut and run, after he let wolves take our cattle," a red-faced, black-haired man with a walrus mustache growled angrily. "Just wait 'til I get my mitts on 'im. He won't look the same once I'm done with 'im."

Nellie stayed clear of her father's line of sight. She knew he would send her away if he saw her there, but she wanted to get near to see what the men were looking at on the ground. Between the milling bodies, she picked out the frayed remains of hemp rope. Picketing stakes pulled up out of the black earth—some only halfway—and a mess of cloven hoof prints.

But what made her spine tingle was the sight of paw prints. Each one seemed almost as big as her hand, and there were hundreds of them, neatly imprinted alongside those of the cattle. The claw marks were clearly visible at the tip of each of the four toes, arranged symmetrically around the center pad.

"Are you sure Norman deserted us?" Nellie heard her father ask.

"Well, we ain't seen hide nor hair of him since we woke up to find this," came the irate response. "And his horse is gone, too."

"Here are hoof prints!" another voice cried out.

Nellie turned to see a younger man, the one who had ridden along with their absconded leader, George Barker, pointing at the ground a way off.

"What do ya mean?" the man with the walrus mustache grunted. "There are hoof prints everywhere."

"No, these belong to a horse, and they're following the trail the cattle left," the young man replied.

"Every man with a horse get saddled up and bring your lariats," Landon commanded, his voice taking on the ring of authority it always did when he was taking charge of a situation.

The men quickly dispersed, soon to be gathered on horseback, their mounts jumpy as a cat on a hot tin roof as they sensed their riders' agitation.

Nellie watched them ride away, wishing she could join in the hunt for the missing Norman and the cattle. As she watched them ride off, an arm hung itself over her shoulders. She felt herself jump with surprise and looked up into her brother Matt's face. He was staring into the distance, following the group of riders with his eyes.

"Shouldn't you be making mud cakes, or something?" he asked, the corner of his mouth twitching as he spoke. "Or helping Ma with breakfast?"

"Oh, Matt!" Nellie blustered at him. "Can't I have even a little fun?"

"A little? I'd say you've been busting at the seams with fun since we left. Gadding about in the meadows, sleeping under the wagon instead of inside it. If Pa finds out, he'll give you what for, and that's no lie."

"But he won't find out 'cause you will not tell him," Nellie lobbed back at him, giving her brother's waist a squeeze that conveyed both affection and a little warning.

"Why'd they let the cattle sleep outside the wagon circle, anyway?" she asked as Matt turned her around and they walked arm in arm back to their wagon, where Anna and Louise were getting a fire pit going.

"Some folks figure they know better than the folks who've been doing this for years, I suppose," her brother replied with a little shrug. "Let's hope they learned their lesson."

"And what about the Norman fellow? Wasn't he supposed to watch them?" Nellie continued her questioning as they reached their families, busy with their usual joint meal preparations.

"He was," Brady answered Nellie's question in Matt's stead. "And he'll be walking beside his horse all the way today, if they find him."

"What if the wolves got him, too?" Nellie enquired further.

"We'll worry about that when the men come back, Nell," her mother replied, handing her a bowl full of unmixed pan bread ingredients. "Now make yourself useful and mix that through for me. Be sure to add more flour if you need to, and don't add too much water, mind, there's already some buttermilk in it from the churning yesterday."

"I'm glad Pa kept our Ivy and the oxen inside the circle," Nellie went on speaking as she glanced over at the cattle still left that had been corralled in the safety of the wagon circle.

"So am I, buttercup, so am I," Anna agreed warmly. "And when you're done with that, go wash up at the spring and comb your hair, you look like a forest nymph who got dragged through a bush backward."

"Yes, Mama," Nellie replied with a giggle and then turned her attention immediately back to Brady while she mixed the bowl of flour, salt, buttermilk and baking soda. "Do you think they'll find Norman and the cattle, Brady?"

"Who knows?" Brady shrugged. "Could be they're all over the prairie by now, like as not."

Nellie finished mixing the dough and handed it back to her mother. Then she ducked into the wagon, hastily picked out her cleanest dirty dress, and grabbed the makings for a quick wash downstream from the spring. She skipped to Alcove Spring, her head buzzing with excitement. She wanted to be done with all the dreary necessities. She wanted to be in on the action when the men came back. The thought of missing any of the excitement was too much to bear.

"I'll bet Norman chased after those wolves all over the prairie until he shot them, every one, and now he's gathering the cattle to bring them back home. And we'll have wolf pelts to keep us warm when we get to the Rocky Mountains and it's freezing," she nattered away to herself as she hastily washed. Then she dressed herself among a cluster of chokecherry bushes, the sweet scent of the tiny white flowers filling her nostrils.

"Hey, fellers! We've got 'em!" a cheerful voice carried over to her on the wind.

"Most of 'em!" another added with a tinge of irony in it.

Nellie grabbed her damp nightdress and scampered from the bushes, leaving the last few buttons on the back of her dress undone. She would see to those later. There were much more important things afoot. As she reached the top of the spring, she could see Landon riding with four brown cattle trotting ahead of him, lowing as they shambled along.

Behind him were more riders, some she did not know, and one who rode a big black horse with a long, flowing mane. He looked grim and a little sheepish, but his face caught her attention immediately. *That's Norman,* she thought, holding her breath. *I remember now. He's the feller riding with the Southey outfit. I think Maddie said he's her cousin.*

A little flutter rose in her stomach. He looked so handsome, as tired and disheveled as he was, with his morning stubble darkening his lower jaw and his black, wavy locks flopping across his face in time to his horse's gait. Nellie hurried across to where the men were once more securing the cattle, but she hugged the line of wagons, ducking behind them as she went to keep from being seen by her father.

"I know, I know," Landon's voice came through clearly as she reached the wagon nearest the men. "You figured to give the cattle more grass to graze, but that ain't a reason to fall asleep. Fact that you went after them yourself to fetch them don't bring back the three steers we lost. I'm just wondering why the blazes you didn't wake the rest of us instead of goin' off on your own. That was even more beef headed than fallin' asleep on watch in the first place."

"I reckon I just wasn't thinkin', sir," Norman confessed, his voice gruff and filled with repentance. "I surely learned my lesson though, and I'll pay the losses for those we couldn't get back."

"Darn right, you will," Landon replied gruffly. "And you'll be walkin' beside your horse today. That's all I have t' say about that."

"Yes, sir," Norman conceded humbly.

Nellie promptly decided to keep him company, at least some of the way. At least then the day's journey wouldn't seem that hard to him. Still hugging her damp nightdress to her chest, she sneaked around to her family's wagon and laid out the nightdress to dry on the wagon seat. Everyone was already sitting around the fire pit, tucking into their breakfast of bacon, eggs, and cornbread.

"Whatever took you so long, Nellie?" her father asked. "Ma said you went off to wash ages ago."

"Oh, nothing," Nellie replied, "I just got distracted by… things." She took her place beside Matt and accepted the tin plate full of food that her mother handed to her.

"Well, then, you'll be helping me wash up today, while the others are free to go when we're done," her mother stated matter-of-factly.

"Yes, Ma," Nellie agreed, trying not to grimace. She wolfed down her breakfast, then rushed to get the plates and cups washed and stowed away. As soon as the circle of wagons began straightening into a line, once again leading with the wagon that had been in the rear the previous day, Nellie kept her eye on the Southeys' rig. Norman was there, walking dutifully beside his horse.

Nellie waited until they were moving steadily away from Alcove Spring before she skipped nonchalantly his way along the row of wagons and then paused, as if just realizing something.

"You're Norman, aren't you?" she queried, screwing up her eyes and tilting her head to one side as she fell in step alongside him.

"Yeah, I am," he replied simply. "Who are you?"

"Nellie," she replied. "My pa is Clyde Henderson." She wasn't sure why she had added that bit of information, but it was too late to unsay it.

"Ah, the feller Landon made second in charge," Norman said, his expression unreadable.

"Uh-huh," Nellie replied. "I'm awfully sorry you have to walk all the way today. If you like, I could keep you company."

"Oh, it's nothin'." Norman waved off her commiseration. "I reckon I would have walked anyway. Hercules deserves his rest. He worked darned hard for me this mornin' and no mistake."

Nellie smiled. "You know, I knew you hadn't deserted us," she said confidently. "I knew you'd gone to find those cows."

Norman blinked and cleared his throat. "You did? But you don't even know me from Adam," he protested, looking a little embarrassed.

"Ma says I have a gift for knowing good folks from bad folks," Nellie countered blithely and then promptly changed the subject. "Did you say your horse's name is Hercules?"

"Uh, yeah, that's his name all right," Norman confirmed, still looking a little self-conscious.

"So you know about Greek mythology, then?"

"Know about it?" he replied. "I love it! Andromeda and Perseus, Pegasus and the Kraken, Medusa, Odysseus… they're epic tales, all of them!"

Nellie couldn't believe her luck. She cracked Norman a grin. "Just so happens, I know a bit about it, too."

The hours seemed to melt away as the sun climbed steadily higher into the sky and the two companions chattered on about fanciful things far removed from their current circumstances. At noon, Nellie dragged herself away from his side and joined her family for lunch. But as soon as the meal was done and the train back on the trail, she was back at Norman's side.

They were so engrossed in their flights of fancy that they scarcely noticed the rapidly darkening sky and the chilly, whipping breeze that picked up around them. Until Landon came riding down the line of wagons, shouting instructions.

"If you have India rubber, better get it out now, you're goin' t' need it. Don't bother with tents, they'll be blown away, anyhow. We got us a ripper comin'."

The cry rose up, "Circle the wagons! Get the cattle inside!"

"I'd better go help," Norman said grimly. "Make up for last night's shenanigans."

Nellie nodded and hurried back to her parents' wagon. She clutched her arms and shivered, suddenly realizing how cold it had gotten, and eyed the menacing black clouds that seemed to churn above them like a live thing. She had just reached her family when the needle-sharp, icy cold raindrops pelted the exposed skin of her hands and face, driven by a howling wind that made the nightly wolf calls they had heard along the trail sound like a lullaby.

Huddling inside the wagon, seated atop crates, trunks, and barrels with the hard surfaces softened by blankets, they waited for the storm to subside. But it was in no hurry to move along. At first, thunder rolled around in the heavens and bright flashes of lightning pierced the gloomy darkness that had descended so quickly on the bright and balmy afternoon. After a while, though, only the insistent patter of rain could be heard and the gurgling of little rivulets forming beneath the wagon.

The hours dragged by with no sign of the storm passing, and even Nellie ran out of games to play. She watched her father peering past the India rubber tarpaulin he had fastened across the front of the wagon cover to keep the rain from blowing in at the opening in the canvas.

"Looks like we should just try to get some shut-eye," he said with a sigh. "This storm's made itself at home here, if you ask me."

"I'm hungry, Pa," Tess whined, leaning against her mother's chest.

Clyde gave Anna a despairing glance.

"We have some dried fruit, still, I think," Anna said, her voice sounding determinedly bright. "And there's a bit of pan bread left from this nooning."

"And milk in the can," Billy added, leaning over and lifting the lid of the steel receptacle.

"So there is," Anna replied. "Nell, won't you and Matt do the honors for us?"

It felt like a bit of an adventure for the moment, but when Nellie awoke in the morning, it was still raining. Hard. Large drops pattered relentlessly on the oiled canvas of their wagon cover.

"How is it possible for so much rain to keep falling from the sky?" she muttered to nobody in particular. Scooching over to the entrance of the wagon cover, she lifted the India rubber tarpaulin and peered outside.

The cattle stood bunched in the middle of the wagon circle, huddled together for warmth, their coats dark with the wetness. Here and there, a family had stretched a tarp or a tent canvas as a makeshift awning beside their wagons and were trying to start cook fires perched on rocks they had dragged under their shelters.

"Look, Pa!" Nellie said, lifting the flap higher and pointing out at the other families. "Can we go outside, too?"

Her father peered past her. "If you don't mind helping me and getting wet, we can do that," he agreed, shrugging.

"I'll help, too!" Billy offered, his voice groggy with sleep but his eyes already brightening at the prospect of a break in the monotony.

Much to Nellie's delight, they soon had their own little awning up, with the rain cascading over it like a small waterfall. She was cold and wet, but she didn't care. It was better than being cooped up in the wagon, sitting on hard wooden crates in cramped conditions. Matt insisted on trying to get the fire going, and Billy jumped in to help him.

"Why don't you play for us a bit, Pa?" Nellie asked, tugging at her father's sleeve. "I think we could all do with a bit of cheering up, right now." Clyde nodded, and she ducked her head under the canvas wagon cover. "Hand over Pa's fiddle there, Tess," she said briskly.

"Oh, all right," Tess grumbled, "but I don't think music is going to make the rain stop."

"May as well cheer ourselves up, then, hadn't we?" Nellie said with a wink at her little sister.

Tess muttered something unintelligible as she handed over the musical instrument and huddled deeper into the blankets she had wrapped herself in.

Nellie passed the fiddle to her father, and after a quick tuning of the strings, he began to play. Nellie sat on the front wheel of their prairie schooner and ignored the bone-chilling, wet cold seeping through her clothes. She closed her eyes as the first sweet strains of a folk song played. She tried to remember what the words were, and then her eyes flew open as the sweetest voice she had ever heard sang.

O the summer time has come
And the trees are sweetly bloomin'
The wild mountain thyme
Grows around the bloomin' heather
Will ye go, lassie, go?

Chapter 5
The Tanners

Matt looked up from striking the flint against the few strands of dry hay and the page of an old newspaper he had requisitioned for kindling. A young woman with rich auburn hair loosely tied back and a milk-white, heart-shaped face was singing in a voice that Matt was sure belonged to an angel.

And we'll all go together
To pull wild mountain thyme
All around the bloomin' heather
Will ye go, lassie, go?

The woman looked up and smiled, though she didn't stop singing. Matt cleared his throat and looked over at his father, who winked at him and went on fiddling, changing from the melody to a sonorous harmony that rose and fell in mesmerizing waves alongside the woman's lilting, soaring voice.

Billy stopped drying the rock he had found to build the fire on for a moment and stared at the woman as well. Nellie jumped down from the front wagon wheel and began dancing a slow and pensive dance around her father and brothers in the already cramped space under the tarpaulin.

Matt turned his focus back to the fire he was trying to build, but his ears were still attentive to the voice ringing from the rig beside his family's.

I will build my love a bower
By yon cool crystal fountain
And 'round it I will pile
All the wild flowers o' the mountain
Will ye go, lassie, go?

Suddenly a movement caught his eye, just as the kindling burst into flame and he shifted it niftily under the wood Billy was stacking on his partially dry rock. The sound of a banjo joined the strains of the violin and the voice, adding a complex rhythmic line supporting the plaintive strains of the song. As the wood crackled and smoked and burst into full flame, the song ended and a hush hung over the little group. Matt looked across to the woman and saw a brown-haired man was sitting beside her, the banjo held casually in his grasp, as if he had been born holding it.

"Can we have something a little happier?" Tessie's voice cut into the breathless silence as her head appeared, all disheveled from beneath the wagon canvas.

"Sure we can, lass," the woman with the angelic voice called out cheerfully, her speech sounding as musical as her singing. "Noel, why don't you give us a little round of 'Drowsy Maggie,' then? I'm sure the little girl would love that one."

She gave Matt a wink, and he felt himself flush. He glanced back down at the fire and needlessly helped Billy, who scowled at him for doing so.

The man with the banjo plucked a few strings and then burst forth with a rollicking tune that instantly had both Matt's and Billy's feet tapping. The next moment, their father's fiddle joined in, his bow dancing across the strings like it was possessed, and the pulsing, rousing melody rose around them. Matt felt as if the music itself was lifting him to his feet.

Nellie gave a little shriek of excitement and clapped her hands together. "Oh! This is what I'm talking about!" she exclaimed, launching into an energetic dance that took her out from under the protective tarpaulin and into the pouring rain. Before he knew what he was doing, Matt felt a guffaw rise in his throat as he joined his sister in her madness.

"Matt! Nellie! You'll catch your death of cold!" Anna cried out, but she could say nothing to stop them. Even Tessie's face had been transformed, and soon she and Billy joined their older siblings, taking hands and spinning around in a circle, first one way and then the other, their feet squelching and splashing on the waterlogged ground.

Suddenly a shriek came from the wagon on the other side of them, and Lucy joined in the fray, linking hands with the Henderson children. Moments behind her, Carrie and then Brady joined in as the music played faster and faster until they were whirling around at a frenzied pace, laughing and yelling in unfettered abandon.

As if their dancing had called its name, the sun broke through the clouds, turning the raindrops into hundreds of falling stars showering all around them. The banjo branched off into a new ditty, and the fiddle followed. More children joined to the horrified cries of their respective parents.

A little red-headed girl who could not have been over three, rushed from the wagon of their musical neighbors and tried to join in the fun, but the auburn-haired songbird rushed forward and hoisted her up onto her hip, dancing with her instead.

Slowly, the rain grew less, and the sun warmed the happy dancers. With one last flourish of a grand finale, the two musicians concluded their song, and the group came to a staggering, giggling, huffing standstill.

"Oh, my! That's just what the doctor ordered," Nellie declared happily, brushing away soggy strands of hair that were clinging to her face.

"I think there are some mothers who'll take a little more convincing than that," her father commented wryly.

"But look!" Billy piped up. "The sun came out to dance, too."

"And about time," Landon's voice interjected.

"Do we have to leave now, Mr. Morland?" Billy asked, his eyes already wide with anticipated disappointment.

"No, not yet, little feller," Landon assured him. "Those wagon wheels'll do more slippin' and slidin' than rollin' on this soggy prairie." He stomped one heavy boot on the ground beneath his feet, kicking up a spray of muddy water and clearly illustrating his point. "Besides, the oxen won't be able t' get a proper foothold. We don't want injured draft animals this early in the journey."

"So we'll just have to cut our losses, then?" Clyde asked.

"Yup," Landon agreed. "We'll see what it's like after noonin'."

Matt looked from one to the other as they spoke, aware he was still holding on to Carrie's hand.

She gently drew it away and smiled up at him. "You're stronger than you look, Matt," she said, her dimple dancing in and out of her cheek.

Matt felt his face grow hot and was sure it must be deep purple, never mind red. "I... um... thank you, Carrie," he stuttered, and looked down at his hands in front of him.

"Well, mister, you sure play a fine fiddle," an unfamiliar voice broke in on Matt's musings as Carrie stepped away, moving toward her beckoning mother in the Morlands' wagon. He turned to see the brown-haired banjo player standing with his feet splayed out at a rakish angle and his arms folded across his chest. A toothy smile adorned his mustached face, although if one wasn't studying him—as an artist like Matt was wont to do to all the strangers he met— one might miss the mustache altogether.

"Thank you, friend," Clyde responded, inclining his head. "I have to say you sure tickled some toes with that banjo of yours."

"Name's Noel Tanner," the banjo player said as the auburn-haired singer stepped closer. "And this is my wife, Dearbhla."

"Dur... vela?" Matt repeated cautiously. "That's an unusual name."

"Dervla," the woman corrected him in her singsong voice. "It's as Irish as potatoes, as I'm sure you've already guessed. Me da gave me that name and taught me every Irish ditty he knows. He made sure I didn't forget my roots, and there's the truth."

"Me, Fee," the little girl on Dearbhla's hip chimed in, her round cheeks flushed and framed with damp red ringlets.

"Aye," Dearbhla laughed. "This is Fiona, our little girl."

"Our pride and joy," Noel added, beaming at her.

"And we've another on the way," Dearbhla added, her hand moving instinctively to the pronounced bump at her midriff that Matt suddenly realized was acting almost as a seat for Fiona.

"Oh, my! You're brave to hit the trail with a baby on the way!" Matt's mother materialized beside him as if out of nowhere.

"Well, we had little choice," Noel said, shrugging.

"Why don't you folks join us for breakfast, and you can tell us all about it," Anna said. "Matt, Billy, get something for our friends to sit on. Nellie and I will take care of the food. Tess, come keep little Fiona busy. Show her some of your toys." She was bustling about while she spoke, motioning with her hands even as the top half of her body disappeared under the wagon cover, opening barrels and chests for the makings of breakfast.

"Don't bother refusing," Matt whispered to their guests. "She don't take no for an answer."

"I heard that, Matt," Anna's muffled voice filtered through the thick canvas.

"Of course you did, Ma," Matt replied playfully, and took off to join Billy in finding a half-decent, half-dry seat for their guests. There weren't many pickings, but they managed to find an old log and rolled it all the way to the wagon. With the India rubber tarp folded over, dry sides facing outward, and placed carefully on top, it made a decent seat for four people.

The meal was almost ready by the time they returned, and they could hear Fiona busily chattering away inside the wagon. Tessa's tired voice punctuated what seemed to be a flood of questions with an occasional half-hearted answer.

"So… tell us what brings you to the trail with a bun in the oven," Anna prodded. Clyde gave his wife a sharp glance. "I must just let you know that I have training as a nurse, so you are more than welcome to call on me if you're ever in any trouble," she added.

"Thank you, kindly, Mrs. Henderson," Dearbhla replied, nodding. Then she turned to her husband. "Shall I tell the story?" she asked. "I know you don't like me interrupting you with details like I usually do." She gave him a radiant smile, and he nodded, looking pleasantly amused.

"Noel and I met and fell madly in love while he was with his father on business in Boston. Me da was a tough nut to convince, but eventually he gave in and let me marry this wonderful man." She looked up at him, her eyes full of adoration.

Matt wondered if Carrie would ever look at him that way and flushed hot, feeling as if everyone could clearly hear the thoughts in his head. He focused on the bacon on his plate and listened to the rest of Dearbhla's story, enjoying the lilt her accent gave the words.

"Noel's da, well, he wasn't the sprightliest, if ye know what I mean. Soon after we were married, and we moved out to the farm, he and Noel's mammie were drivin' home from market, and he keeled over suddenly, clutchin' at his chest. The wagon near crashed into a ditch, but his wife took over the reins and saved her own life. It was too late to do anything about his."

She gripped Noel's hand. "Poor soul died of a broken heart herself, I swear it. I've never seen a person go down so fast. She became a shadow within a few weeks, and then she was gone."

Matt wondered at Dearbhla's description. It was so poetic, he could almost imagine an oil painting of the disappearing lady.

"Anyhow, we went on as best we could, but without Noel's da t' guide us, we were just flounderin', and there's the truth of it. We kept loanin' money, tryin' our best t' get a crop out of the ground, but there was just no givin'. In the end, we had t' sell and had no money left for startin' fresh, so we figured we'd take a ride across country, get us a little patch of land for nothin', and have an adventure in the process."

She beamed round at the party and took a bite of cornbread, clearly showing her tale was told.

"I've also heard there's gold to be had in the Sierra Nevada," Noel added, his face bright with hope. "If I can get myself a few nuggets there, we can build ourselves a real cozy place in Oregon and maybe try our hand at cattle farmin'. I've about figured I ain't much for crops. Maybe I'll plant a little alfalfa for the beeves, but other than that, I'll be fine and dandy just lettin' 'em graze."

Matt thought long and hard about the Tanners while the hot sun beat down and the wagons rolled further west after nooning. He walked beside his family's wagon and listened to the sound of Dearbhla's voice behind him, accompanied by Fiona's high, childish tones chiming in every so often. They seemed nice enough, but he felt like there was something they weren't telling the whole truth about.

His thoughts wandered ahead to the Morlands' wagon, and he stepped up his pace, lengthening his strides so he could walk beside Carrie and Helen. He made sure to place Helen between himself and Carrie. The fear of accidentally brushing her hand with his and making her think he had improper intentions was a risk he was not willing to take. "Hello, girls," he said with affected nonchalance as he came alongside the two sisters.

"We're ladies to you, young man," Helen retorted, looking down her nose at him. "And if you're looking for Brady, we don't know where he is. Probably up ahead, scouting with Papa."

"Oh, I'm sure I wouldn't want to interrupt them," Matt said, uncertain what else to say. He had never been one for society, and what he knew about polite conversation was almost dangerous.

"Of course you wouldn't," Helen replied scornfully. "But you seem perfectly happy to interrupt us."

"Oh, come now, Helen," Carrie chided gently. "It's not like we were having any kind of important conversation."

"It was important to me," Helen insisted. "Papa is talking about not waiting on mail if there's nothing from Isabella when we get there. I know for a fact she will have written by now and made sure the letter reaches me. I told her what Papa said about us reaching Fort Kearny in about three weeks. She'll have sent something along with time enough to spare. Perhaps even a parcel with some kind of creature comfort to distract me from these endless swarms of flies and mosquitoes and the maddeningly chirruping bugs, whatever they're called."

"Cicadas," Matt stated, trying to be helpful. All he got for his efforts was a withering glare.

"I really don't care what they're called, you know?" Helen informed him. "Something that hideous and raucous shouldn't even have a name. And my feet are killing me, and I can't even ride in the wagon. Tell me, what good is a wagon if you can't ride in it?"

"You know full well why we can't ride in the wagon, Helen," Carrie reminded her gently but firmly. "You're just tired. You'll feel better after a good night's rest."

Helen stopped dead in her tracks. "A good night's rest? How am I supposed to have that with blood-sucking, whining mosquitoes as big as turkeys buzzing around my head all night? And I resent you belittling my suffering."

"Not belittling, Helen dear." Carrie soothed her sister's scratchy feelings with her incomparable smile. "Just trying to encourage you. It's getting late, and soon we'll be setting up camp again. No more walking for a while."

"Yes, and then it'll be making fire and cooking and cleaning and trying to find a comfortable spot on a wagon full of uncomfortable spots. A fine bit of encouragement, that is," Helen fussed, refusing to have her spirits lifted.

Matt wondered at Carrie's apparently bottomless supply of patience in the face of Helen's determined murmuring, and decided he liked her even more than before. "So we're almost at Fort Kearny, then?" he asked, wanting the conversation to continue, if only to have Carrie's warm, slightly husky tones caressing his ear.

"Pa says we should roll in there tomorrow or the next day, if we don't have any holdups like yesterday's storm," Carrie replied.

"We'd better not or I swear I'll take a horse and ride back to Independence like Mr. Barker did." Helen sulked and then stalked off ahead of them, clearly tired of their company.

"Don't mind her," Carrie said softly in her sister's wake. "She's always been the sensitive one of us. I honestly don't know where she came from sometimes. But we still love her."

"I suppose she'll get used to life on the trail eventually," Matt added hopefully.

"Either that or we'll all go stark raving mad with her around," Carrie laughed.

Chapter 6
Fort Kearny

Fort Kearny was not the fortified military post Matt had envisioned in his mind. The square of simple adobe buildings surrounding a dusty center plaza, lined with a row of young cottonwood trees, was populated by a milling crowd that contained many people. Some of them were familiar to Matt, at least in their dress and mannerisms, while others were wholly strange to him.

Besides the soldiers in their rather shabby, ill-fitting gray uniforms, there were trappers and hunters, Indians with shaved heads and some with braids, peddlers and merchants—overdressed and loud-mouthed—men with felt hats and braces holding up their grubby shirts over their equally grubby pants, and ladies in feathers and some in calico, but most of them wearing gingham dresses like Carrie's.

"You'll have to report to Lieutenant Colonel Bonneville," a young, fresh-faced soldier told Matt's father after he asked who was in charge of the fort. "He'll help you with supplies as well. At good prices." He leaned in closer and whispered conspiratorially, "Trust me, these other fellers will fleece you naked if you give 'em half a chance." He stepped back and nodded, apparently satisfied he had saved at least one wagon train from the greed of the local merchants.

"Thank you, Private," Landon said, giving the young man a hearty slap on the back.

With that, they stepped in the direction the soldier had pointed. But they were not prepared for what they heard next.

Matt hung back as his father and Landon Morland stepped through the doorway of the building the young soldier had directed them to.

Brady stepped over the threshold, and then looked back as he noticed Matt's hesitation out of the corner of his eye. "Ain't you comin', Matt?" he asked, looking surprised.

"I figured it was for our pas to take care of," Matt replied uncertainly.

Landon's head appeared over Brady's shoulder. "It'll be good for ya t' listen in. Ain't no tellin' what might happen out here. Who knows? Next time, you young fellers might need to take over from us."

Matt wasn't quite sure what Landon meant by that, but he trusted the older and far more experienced man's judgment. He stepped inside behind Brady and let his eyes adjust to the dimness of the room. Slowly, he made out an interior that was far more luxurious than what the outside of the building had led him to imagine.

The walls had been whitewashed. Woven leather rugs decorated with bright beads covered the earthen floor. Thick pelts of bear, wolf, and bison hung resplendent over solid wooden chairs, carved with intricate detail. Maps, stuffed animal heads, swords, and portraits adorned the walls.

A dark-haired gentleman sat behind a large wooden desk, his eyes riveted to a sheet of paper he was writing on. "Sit down," he commanded, without looking up.

The four each helped themselves to a seat and waited. After a few moments more of the pen nib scratching the rough paper, the lieutenant colonel signed it with a flourish, doused the page with salt, and intertwined his fingers into each other as he leaned his forearms on the desk and looked up at his visitors.

"You've just come in on a wagon train?" he barked. Matt could tell his name had not belied his lineage. A thick French accent colored his words.

"That's right," Landon confirmed. "There's thirteen wagons in the train. Most of us families lookin' for a new life in Oregon."

"Is that so?" the man replied, his down-turned mouth corners twitching slightly. He was uncharacteristically clean shaven for a man of his age and stature—Matt guessed he was in his early fifties. His pointed nose reminded Matt of a crow's beak, and his eyes, dark and glittering, peered suspiciously out from between narrowed lids surrounded by sagging, puffy skin. "Well, I hope you find it, or at least, the few of you who make it that far."

Matt saw the two wagon train leaders exchange a glance. His father twirled his hat in his hands, and Landon sat up a little straighter. "One of your soldiers told us we should request supplies from you rather than the merchants," he said, clearly choosing to ignore Bonneville's pessimistic comment.

The lieutenant colonel leaned back in his bearskin-draped chair and folded his arms across his chest. "Oui, I will do that, but first I will do my best to stop you from making the mistake of your lives," he stated without drama. But the dourness of his tone stirred a sense of alarm in Matt.

"Now, that's mighty thoughtful of ya, Lieutenant Colonel," Landon countered, lifting a hand, "but I'd rather you don't fret yourself about our safety. We ain't greenhorns. We know what we're lettin' ourselves in for, and we're willin' t' take the risks."

"Ça alors!" One eyebrow on the commanding officer's unwelcoming face lifted. "So you will expose your wives and children to being scalped by savages, run over by wagons, trampled and mauled by both domestic and wild beasts, drowned in swollen rivers, shot to death accidentally by fools who cannot use a rifle properly, and bitten by rattlesnakes! To say nosing of the plagues of dysentery, cholera, and typhoid fever! That is wonderful to know!" The man's cheeks shivered with urgency as he leaned forward in his seat. His black eyes seemed to pop out of their sockets as he spoke, flecks of spittle forming on his lips.

"By all accounts, I've heard the tribes have been more helpful than hostile to folks who don't go crawlin' their hump. As for the rest, we're aware of the dangers. Thank you, Lieutenant Colonel. Now, if you don't mind, we'd like t' get our supplies refreshed. Especially grain for the horses." Landon spoke calmly, his voice soothing the chaos that Bonneville's words had awakened in Matt's mind.

Bonneville leaned back once more, his fingertips pressed together under his chin. "Don't say I didn't warn you," he said blankly, and picked up his pen once again. Taking a clean sheet of paper from a sheaf on his desk, he wrote with a flourish and a grunt, signed the note, and lit the seal wax in his stationery tray by dipping the wick in the flame of an oil lamp that stood on his desk. Pressing his ring into the hot wax that he dribbled on the page, he blew over it a few times and then held it out to Landon. "Get what you need, take your rest, and I wish you good luck," he said. "Zut! You'll need it."

"Much obliged, Lieutenant Colonel," Landon said, rising from his seat and taking the official letter.

Bonneville grunted and fluttered his fingers in the door's direction.

Matt quickly stepped outside and looked up at the two older men's faces as they emerged from what seemed like a cave of doom and gloom in Matt's mind. "Pa, is it true what he said," he asked, trying not to sound scared. "There's that many things that can kill us out here?"

Clyde Henderson shrugged. "I suppose, but we've come this far, haven't we? And we know there're folks who have made it all the way alive, don't we?"

"I guess so," Matt agreed, not feeling fully convinced.

"Your pa's right, Matt," Landon chipped in. "And so is Bonneville, bless his heart. Fact is, we can't turn around now. We've left our lives behind already. May as well finish what we started."

"Did you mean what you said about the Indians, Mr. Morland?" Matt queried, seeking one last scrap of reassurance.

"I sure did. I know we had us a little scare soon out of Independence, but, hey, we all came out alive, didn't we? Best thing you can do is keep a cool head, son. Whether it's an Indian you're facin', or a bear, or a bad bout of dysentery. More folks go belly up losin' their heads than anything else, and that's the honest truth." Landon's eyes smiled, even though his mouth was still firm and grim as ever.

"Yeah," Brady agreed with his father. "Long as we don't go crawlin' their humps, like you said, Pa, they'll leave us alone."

"Hmmm…" Landon said pensively. "We better hope it stays that way. From what I've been hearin', them forty-niners have been makin' a nuisance of themselves, huntin' Indians for no reason and makin' them distrustful of anyone with a pale face."

Matt swallowed. His father had warned his entire family of the dangers. At first, during their early days on the trail, he had decided they were mostly myths or isolated incidents, designed to scare folks away from striking out to find a new beginning. But now they were looking more real than he could ever have imagined.

He tried to focus on the task at hand as the men went from store to store, buying the supplies they needed for their train. Flour and sugar, coffee and tea, bacon and lard. There were no dried peaches or apples, but there was some rice. They brought the wagons, lining up for their provisions to be loaded, and Matt and Brady helped the older men measure out each one's share.

"You reckon I'm any good with a rifle, now, Brady?" Matt asked. "I mean, I'm sure you taught me well, I'm just wondering if you think I'd be able to protect my family if needs be."

"Well, you shoot a little better than Carrie, so I reckon that's sayin' somethin'," Brady remarked.

"Carrie can shoot?" Matt felt his jaw drop.

"She sure can," Brady laughed, pouring a bag of rice into a barrel on the Southey wagon. "She'd never tell a soul, so don't go sayin' I told you. Ma isn't very happy about it, but she knows Pa wouldn't teach her any less well than he taught me."

"Why wouldn't she tell anyone?" Matt wondered out loud. "Seems to me like a pretty remarkable skill for a lady to have."

"Fellers don't like a woman who can protect herself," Brady replied with a wink. "Long as they think she's helpless and needin' their protection, she'll be more likely t' find herself a beau."

"She doesn't have a beau waiting in Columbia?" Matt asked, hoping Brady would say no.

"A whole lot of 'em, but I don't reckon any of 'em's got a snowball's chance in hell, anyway," Brady quipped with a grin.

Matt hoped he wasn't blushing as red as he felt. He also hoped Brady wasn't aware of his interest in Carrie. Especially after that last comment. She was obviously a popular young woman, and for good reason. Matt sighed quietly to himself as he hoisted a bag of flour onto his shoulder and headed for his family's wagon. He would do well to let the dream go. If only she weren't so perfect.

***

Two days later, when the wagon train creaked and rattled its way out of the Fort Kearny area, he still hadn't shaken the butterflies in his stomach whenever she was around. He tried not to watch her walking ahead of him, beside her father's cattle, cracking a long whip now and then to keep the lumbering beasts from wandering too far off the trail.

The prairie had become flatter, and the trees had thinned to almost nothing. It felt like they were wading through a sea of grass and sky and sun. Hardly a breeze stirred. Every footfall stirred some kind of insect, and the only sound, other than the creaking of wagons and plodding footfalls of oxen, mules and horses, was the whirring and buzzing of insects of all shapes, sizes, and colors.

At first, they enthralled Tess and Billy, calling each other over to a new spot every few minutes to see what they had found. With the sun nearing the peak of its slow climb into the sky, they had become tired and listless, the heat and monotony clearly evaporating their earlier joie de vivre.

"Oh, Mr. Morland," Tess groaned, "how long till we get to the river crossing? There's nothing but grass and sky and bugs here."

Matt empathized with his little sister, though he didn't say so out loud. The complete lack of landmarks made it feel like they were walking and walking, but going nowhere. Everything looked and sounded the same, no matter how long they walked.

"Not for another six days at best, little miss," Landon replied without sympathy. "Best make up ways to keep yourself busy, or ya might end up goin' plumb loco."

"The truth of the matter is we were *plumb loco* to go on this trip, anyway. At least I was. I don't know why I didn't stay in Columbia. Isabella told me I could stay with her. Oh, it would have been heavenly compared to this senseless drudgery." Helen's voice cut through the sultry air.

"I reckon I know why you came along, Helen," Landon replied, without giving his daughter as much as a glance. "Because we're your family, and we're more important to you than your comfort."

His tone was not unkind, but his words clearly cut Helen to the core. She opened her mouth to reply and then snapped it shut, straightening her back as she linked her fingers behind her and walked onward in silence. Carrie had moved up ahead, to the Southeys wagon. She and Nellie were walking alongside the man named Norman, who had let the wolves get to the cows that one night.

Matt briefly wondered why Nellie was spending so much time with the young man. He toyed with the idea of joining the little group, but it was not only the heat and thirst that made his tongue stick to the roof of his mouth and convinced him he did not want to be the tongue-tied secret admirer at that particular moment.

After what felt like days of walking, Landon finally called noon, and the wagons circled. Nobody spoke much. They were all tired, hot, and consumed with their own thoughts. The fiddle and banjo lay silent in their respective wagons, but nobody issued a request from either musician.

With their bellies reasonably full, the pioneers sought the sparse shade offered by the wagons' bulk and rested for a while. But all too soon, Landon and Clyde were on their feet again, exhorting their cohorts to brave the afternoon leg of the day's journey. The two strolled along beside the Henderson wagon as soon as travel was underway again, and Matt listened in on their conversation for lack of anything better to do but stare at the unending waves of shimmering prairie grasses.

"We'd best swing a little more north," Landon said, his shrewd eyes scanning the horizon. "We'll need to get to the Platte for water. There's a little stream runs into it here and there, so I've heard, but that's where we'll be sure to get our cattle and ourselves watered. May as well stop there for the night, too."

"No more springs?" Clyde asked, and Matt thought back to the fresh, chilly waters of Alcove Spring.

"Oh, there'll be springs and wells, but if you don't want dead oxen and horses, you'd do well to keep 'em away from those till we get to the river," Landon replied grimly.

"Dead? From water?" Clyde repeated, aghast.

"No, alkali poisoning. It ain't for certain the pools will be tainted, but it ain't for certain they won't either," Landon informed him. Then he turned to Matt. "As a matter of fact, we should make sure the rest of the train knows. Matt, fetch Brady, and you fellers spread the word down the train." He paused. "Or across the train."

His words were not idly chosen. The wagons had fanned out now that there were so many miles of vast prairie stretching out on either side of them. Instead of rumbling along in single file and eating each other's dust, they now advanced along the sea of waving grass like a line of chargers headed into battle.

"Will do, Mr. Morland," Matt agreed, and immediately set off to find Brady.

"And tell them not to get too close to the river with their wagons," Landon called after him.

Matt glanced back and raised a hand in acknowledgement, heading for the first wagon in the line. Brady was not there, but as he went along, he conveyed Landon's message. The overlanders nodded their weary agreement, and if they questioned their leader's advice, none of them said so.

His search for Brady coming up fruitless, Matt completed the mission on his own and returned to his wagon to take over the task of leading the oxen. The blazing heat of the sun had lessened, and a cool breeze blew.

Billy came to walk alongside his brother. "What's that about a river?" he asked.

"We're headed for the Platte," Matt answered, feeling good that he knew something.

"The Platte? Why'd they call it that?"

Matt shrugged. "I don't know."

"It's French for flat." The familiar voice behind Matt made his heart jump into his throat. He swallowed it down quickly and turned to look into the confident, laughing green eyes of Carrie.

"How can a river be flat?" Billy asked, pulling a face.

"I guess we'll have to wait and see," Carrie replied, her dimple deepening as she gave Matt a wink.

He felt his cheeks blazing and looked away to the north, pointing with a finger he was trying hard to keep from shaking. "Your pa says the Platte is that way," he said, thinking how arbitrary his statement sounded.

"I'm going ahead to look," Billy announced and promptly ran off.

"Don't go too far, Billy!" Matt yelled after him.

Billy waved without looking back.

Finding himself alone with Carrie, Matt searched his brain for something to say—hopefully something more intelligent than his last remark—but came up hopelessly empty. They walked on in silence, and he began to feel like she was quite happy to continue that way, as if being beside him was enough. He sneaked a peek at her. She was smiling softly to herself as she gazed over the green sea of grass.

"I see it! I see it!" the thin cry of Billy's shrill voice from far off drifted to them on the winds. In the distance, Matt could see him jumping up and down and waving his arms ecstatically. "It really is flat! And so wide!" He flung his arms out in an effort to portray what he was seeing.

It was only after the river came into sight of the slowly moving wagons that he understood what his little brother meant. As if in competition with the endless prairie, the river seemed to stretch almost to the horizon. Its waters shimmered in the late afternoon sun as it slid across the white and brown sands that seemed to be only a few inches below the surface.

Little elongated islands, the larger ones sporting shrubs and grass polls, the smaller ones boasting only piles of round pebbles, were scattered across its length and breadth. Matt stared in wonderment at the magical-looking river, when, without warning, the leather lariat was ripped from his hand.

He looked up in startled alarm. The oxen were veering off, headed in a hurry for what Matt could not tell.

With a yell, he gave chase, almost stumbling in his efforts to snatch up the lariat. Then he saw it. A pool of water nestled among the grasses. With Landon's words of warning ringing in his ears, Matt pounced on the lariat and hauled back on it with all his weight and strength. "Bacon! Butch! No!"

Chapter 7
The Platte

Billy stared out over the mass of water sparkling in the afternoon sunlight. He had seen nothing like it, and the sight immediately transported him from the dreary days trudging to a world of endless opportunities. He silently wished the wagon train would stay close to the river so he could give some of those opportunities a bash.

A frantic cry split the air behind him, and Billy knew, in that instant, that it was his brother Matt. Spinning around to face back toward the wagon train, he saw Matt leaning back on the oxen's lead rope, yelling at them incoherently. His father and Landon were rushing toward him, obviously intent on helping him drag the cattle away from whatever they were straining to get at.

Billy rushed back toward his family, determined to add his bit of strength for what it was worth. Excitement coursed through his veins, mingled with the thrilling sense of fear and danger. This was more like it! He had almost thought there would be no adventure anymore, just a monotonous trek across the bland, barren countryside.

By the time he reached them, the other men had dragged the lowing, frothing animals away from whatever it was they were straining after.

"Unhitch them while we hold them steady!" Landon yelled to him as he approached.

Billy stared at the chains and metal links of the wagon tongue and yoke. He did not know what to do. His mind was spinning. He knew he had to do something or a tragedy would come upon them, even though in that moment, he had no idea what that tragedy would look like.

"Pull out the pin!" Landon urged. "On top of the yoke!"

Billy's eyes scanned the wood and metal once more, still with no idea what he was looking for. A flash of red and white gingham crossed his vision. And the next moment, Tess brushed past him, holding up the iron pin Landon had clearly referred to. He hadn't even seen where she had pulled it from.

"To the river!" Landon yelled, and the group of men dragged the unwilling oxen toward the waters.

Billy watched them go, wondering why he had let himself be shown up by his little sister. She came to stand beside him, apparently biting her tongue, because she said nothing about what had just happened. Together they watched as the two oxen suddenly realized there was a vast expanse of water before them and almost lifted their escorts off their feet as they trotted eagerly toward the shining river. The men stepped back, shaking their heads and laughing with relief.

"How did you know what pin to pull out?" Billy mumbled, his gaze fixed on the other wagons rolling past them to the beckoning waters so he wouldn't have to look his sister in the eye.

"Papa showed me," Tess said simply. "You know I like these sorts of things. That's why I also put the brake on the wagon so it wouldn't roll away when we got Bacon and Butch loose."

Billy gave a little humph and looked away. He knew she was right.

"You were brave to come running to help, Billy," his mother's voice sounded at his left ear while her soft but strong arm encircled his shoulders.

"I wasn't much use, was I?" he retorted and then immediately regretted it. He had a holy fear of hurting his mother's feelings. She always said nobody was good except God, but he was sure she came pretty close.

"It's your heart that counts," she replied, kissing him on the cheek even as he tried to pull away. "Now, see what you can do to help the other settlers. Perhaps they can use someone as helpful as you are."

***

Her words echoed in Billy's mind as the days dragged on and the settlers traveled west of northwest along the wide Platte River. He really wanted to be helpful. Partly because his mother wanted it so, and partly because it kept his mind occupied. With no more rock outcrops and cottonwood groves to offer hours of exploration and intrigue, his mind—and his hands—had grown restless.

He had not forgotten his pledge to his father before they left Philadelphia. *I promise, Pa. No pranks and no teasing my sisters.* The words came back to haunt him. He bit his lip and looked up at the cloudless blue sky. Even the river had lost its initial allure. He desperately needed distraction.

He shoved his hands in his pockets and kicked at a grass clump, wondering what he could do next, when a flash of movement caught his eye. Slithering away between the dust and grass was a small snake. It was light dusty brown with a pale, creamy belly and a single stripe of the same color as its belly running down the length of its back from its head to the tip of its tail.

Billy perked up immediately. He couldn't remember what Mr. Morland had called those little snakes, but he knew for certain he had said they were harmless. In a flash, he was on its trail, cutting off its escape route every time. There were no sticks to be had, so it forced him to use only his hands and his wits. Just before he lost sight of the wagon train, he gripped the little reptile behind the head, just as Mr. Morland had also taught him.

Careful not to get his fingers bit, simply because he didn't want anyone to see the cuts and ask about them, he wrapped his find in his handkerchief, tying the ends securely, and stowed it in his pocket. He wasn't sure yet what he was going to do, but he knew something would come to him later. Maybe he could scare Helen with it. She looked like she needed a little excitement in her life, too.

He smiled to himself as he rejoined the wagons, feeling a bit better about the lack of things to keep him busy on the trail. That evening, the wagons circled on the banks of the South Platte, as Landon called it.

"In the mornin' we'll be crossin' over," he declared at the hastily assembled camp meeting before the overlanders went about their nightly chores and routines. "Be warned that the Platte ain't like any other river we've crossed. It's muddy and full of sand banks. We'll try t' find the best places t' cross, and that may take us further south again, but it'll all be worth it t' have a safe crossin'."

He looked around at the assembled pioneers in the slowly waning sunlight. Ben followed his gaze. They looked tired, some of them a little irritated. Not least of them Helen. She was scowling and rubbing one bare foot as she sat on the ground, muttering to herself.

That evening as the families were preparing their meals, the Hendersons, Morlands, and Tanners all joined forces. Billy did his best to be as helpful as he possibly could, jumping up and offering his services whenever one child was called upon by their parents to complete a small task. Across the flickering fire, he caught his mother's eye as she gave him an approving smile.

"Helen, love," Louise Morland addressed her daughter. "I've quite forgotten to fill the salt pot. Won't you be an angel and do it for me?"

Before Helen was done rolling her eyes and taking a breath, ostensibly to inform her mother that the blisters on her feet made it entirely impossible for her to fulfil her mother's request, Billy jumped to his feet. "I'll do it, Mrs. Morland," he offered gallantly. "I know how hard all this walking is on Helen."

The lady under discussion gave him a surprised look, but didn't argue his point.

Helen's mother looked at him keenly for a moment, as if she was pondering whether it was worth indulging her daughter to accept his offer. She seemed to decide and nodded. "All right, thank you, Billy. That's very kind of you,

I'm sure. The salt is in the corner on the left, at the back of the wagon."

Billy stepped forward, taking the cattle horn saltshaker she held out to him, and clambered inside the Morlands' wagon. It seemed to be less crowded with things than theirs was. He located the salt barrel, filled the shaker, and was about to climb out of the wagon when an idea struck him like a lightning bolt. He patted his pocket. The snake was still there. It seemed to enjoy the warmth of his body.

Billy lifted the lid of a nearby barrel. That one was filled with flour. Without taking time to consider what he was doing, Billy drew the snake out of his pocket, untied the corners of his handkerchief, and shook the garter snake out into the barrel before quickly slamming the lid back down.

"Everything all right in there, Billy?" his mother's voice reached his ears.

"It sure is, Ma," he called back and vaulted down to the ground. Quickly, he stepped over to Mrs. Morland and handed her the refilled saltshaker. He flashed a quick smile at Helen, who merely gave him a curt nod before turning her head to stare into the fire. Then he sat down, hardly able to focus on the rest of the conversation as he pictured the excitement that could unfold in a few hours. At least there would be one moment that wasn't dull.

Pa played his fiddle, and Noel Tanner jangled along on his banjo while his pretty wife, Dearbhla, drew a small crowd with her soul-stirring singing voice.

Oh! shrive me, father—haste, haste, and shrive me,
Ere sets yon dread and flaring sun;

Its beams of peace—nay, of sense, deprive me,
Since yet the holy work's undone.
The sage, the wand'rer's anguish balming,
Soothed her heart to rest once more;
And pardon's promise torture calming,
The Pilgrim told her sorrows o'er.

Billy felt a strange compunction that the lyrics of the song were somehow relevant to him, but their words were unfamiliar, almost like a foreign language. He grew drowsy and slept, becoming aware, as if in a dream, of his father's arms lifting him up and carrying him to his bedroll in the wagon.

***

The pioneers were rising groggily in response to the sound of the morning's rousing rifle shot when Billy jumped down from the wagon and stretched, trying to work out the kinks in his spine. It was still dark, with just a faint gloaming of gray in the east. Families all around the circle were starting their breakfast fires and taking their cattle down to the river for a drink when a bloodcurdling scream and a crash ripped through the still morning air.

All heads turned toward the Morlands' wagon. Louise Morland left the fire-making to the other two women and dashed toward the sound.

A white-faced, shaking Helen emerged from the canvas cover, tumbling over the side of the wagon box to fall sobbing helplessly into her mother's arms. "A snake!" she spluttered through her tears. "An awful, evil, deadly snake! I almost died, Ma!"

"Did it bite you, Helen?" her mother asked as the men came rushing closer, abandoning their cattle to the care of the other overlanders.

"I… I… don't think so," Helen stammered. "I can't feel my body, so I wouldn't know if…" She trailed off and then her voice rose again to a fevered pitch. "I can't feel my body! Oh, Mama! I don't want to die! I don't want to die!"

Billy watched the episode with rapt interest, forgetting he was on his way to fetch water from the river so the Henderson family could wash up. "That's funny," he remarked quietly. "Yesterday it sounded to me like she would rather be dead than out here on the prairie." He chuckled softly and watched as Landon Morland clambered hastily into his wagon to emerge moments later with the snake coiled around his arm, his thumb and forefinger deftly gripping it behind the head.

"It ain't nothin' but a garter snake, Helen," he stated flatly. "I'll stake my life on it you've seen at least a dozen of 'em on the ranch in your lifetime." He tossed the snake out into the prairie grass, and it slithered rapidly away, disappearing in seconds.

Helen buried her face in her mother's shoulder and kept sobbing.

Billy covered his mouth and chuckled. The show was getting more entertaining by the second.

"Hey! Billy! Are you going to fetch water or what?" Matt's voice broke into his reverie, startling him back to action.

"I'm going!" he yelled back over his shoulder as he took off running and then yelped as he accidentally banged the bucket against his leg. His eye caught his mother's as he ran by, and he instinctively knew that soon, somewhere along the next day or so, he was going to be subjected to a questioning. He tried not to think about it and made a beeline for the shallow waters of the South Platte, already reflecting the first rosy tinges of the morning sky.

***

"I don't trust this piece of river, here," Landon said thoughtfully, standing near the water's edge and surveying the rippling tide washing over patches of white sand and brown mud. "We should try further down south."

"It'll take longer," Clyde remarked, equally thoughtful. "Won't we lose the same time either way?"

Billy looked from one to the other and folded his arms over his chest, straddling his feet wide as he tried to imitate Landon's stance. The wagon train leader plucked a stalk of prairie grass and chewed it as he shook his head in response to Clyde's question.

"Getting stuck'll tire out the oxen, too. And the mules, well, let's just say they'll be worse hell-raisers than they are already." He tossed the stalk of grass aside and marched back to his wagon. "Tell the others to follow," he said over his shoulder as he headed back to the camp.

Soon the usual cacophony of cracking whips, lowing oxen, and calls of "Wagons, ho!" could be heard rising up from the train. Billy skipped alongside them as they formed a line parallel to the river. Here and there, he noticed things he had not seen before, now illuminated by the morning sun. Discarded items of all kinds, half in and half out of the water.

A trunk with its lid open, emptied of everything except some soggy books. An assortment of cans, all sizes, some opened and empty, some still sealed with their labels peeling off. He picked up a few and shoved them in his pockets. Further down the river, what used to be a beautiful pear wood bureau lay half submerged, its outer layers already bleaching in the merciless prairie wind and sun. Near to it, a rusting wood stove lay on its side, the water swirling around and through it.

It was not long before he found out why those items lay there, seemingly senselessly abandoned. The first six wagons crossed, at the point Landon chose, with a bit of a struggle but safely. The sands were sinking softly and seemed to tug at Billy's feet while he enthusiastically added his weight to the communal efforts of the other menfolk.

Pushing and pulling the wagons through the deepest, mushiest places, he learned that sandbanks often looked deceptively firm until one drove a wagon over them. Also, it was nearly impossible to know how deep the muddier parts of the river were. His back and arms ached with the effort, and his legs felt shaky, but it felt good to be working alongside the men.

The men took a quick rest, and then the other seven wagons entered the water, one by one. They were nearly all across when a cry came to them, across the expanse of rippling, gurgling water. All heads turned downstream in the sound's direction, and everyone sucked in their breath with a collective gasp at the sight that met their eyes.

A wagon lay at a dizzying angle, one front wheel lifting awkwardly into the air. The rear wheel diagonally opposite was submerged deeper than Billy would have imagined possible. One family had clearly been impatient and crossed lower down instead of staying in their spot in line for the day. They stood waving and crying for help, their oxen straining against the oxbows as they frantically tried to free their burden from the sand that was sucking it deeper and deeper.

"We have to help them unload!" Landon shouted. "Brady, get this lot to shore! The rest of you, get everything you can carry out that wagon right away!" He was already leaping like a two-legged gazelle through the water as he shouted commands, headed for the stranded wagon and the terrified draft animals yoked to it.

Billy waded closer as fast as he could and watched the men hoisting barrels, crates, nondescript bundles wrapped in quilts, suitcases, and many tools and household equipment from the wagon box. As he reached the stricken vessel, Landon told him, "Help us push, Billy."

The young man needed no second invitation. As tired and achy as his limbs were, he heaved with all his strength against the wooden box, hearing the shouts of "Hup! Hup! Heave!" as Landon and the wagon's owner—a sandy-haired, bearded fellow he knew only as Arthur—urged the already exhausted oxen to make one last valiant effort.

A sucking, slurping sound erupted beside Billy's feet, and the next moment, the wheel came free as the oxen lurched forward and headed single-mindedly for the opposite bank. Landon and Arthur splashed along beside them, trying to slow the panicky creatures before they floundered into another sinkhole and upset the wagon again.

Billy made his own slow way to shore, even more convinced than ever that if Landon Morland told him to do anything, he would be sure to follow his instructions to the letter. A little twinge of guilt twisted his innards as he thought of the garter snake episode, but he pushed it quickly from his mind as he joined the other pioneers on the bank.

Chapter 8
The Slades

Clyde stood at the top of the steep, rocky hill and let out a low whistle.

"I hear ya," Landon responded gravely.

"We'll need a windlass to get down here," Clyde remarked, his eye scanning the descent that seemed to plummet down at nothing less than forty-five degrees. "It's nearly perpendicular!"

Landon chuckled into his beard. "You could say that," he agreed, the grass stalk between his teeth bobbing up and down as he nodded and pointed to the bottom of the hill. "Whatever we do, we'll have t' make sure everybody works together on this one. We don't want t' end up like those poor shucks."

Clyde swallowed. At the bottom of the steep incline, which seemed about a half mile long, he could vaguely make out the shattered remains of wagons, side by side with the carcasses of a few animals who had not made the journey. Scattered among them, bleached white bones told him this hill had been claiming lives for a long, long time. A somber air settled over both men.

"I guess that's all the warning anybody needs," Clyde commented wryly, and the two men turned to walk back to the waiting wagon train. "You sure it won't be safer to go around it?" he added cautiously, aware by now that Landon was a man who liked to take risks, although not uncalculated ones.

"We could," he replied, shrugging. "If we're fixin' t' lose another… I don't know… day, day-and-a-half, goin' the extra seventeen miles. We already had to stop a little longer yesterday to let the oxen rest."

Clyde didn't think that needed a response. He dug his hands into his pockets and rolled his still aching shoulders back, wondering how he would feel after another bout of extreme physical exertion. He listened carefully while Landon spoke to the gathered travelers.

"We go down one at a time," Landon announced, the tone of his voice leaving no room for argument. "Everyone make sure their brakes ain't broken and do whatever it takes t' get those wheels so they can't roll."

"Can't roll?" the young man named Norman spoke up. "How's that goin' t' help us?"

"Well, I can help you understand that," Clyde replied in Landon's stead. "Those wagons, with their lead weight of freight, plus gravity pulling them, they'll go rolling down that hill faster than the oxen and mules can handle. We'll have to hold them back, too, even with the wheels fixed so they can't roll. If we don't, they'll end up tumbling right over the draft animals and doing a few cartwheels down to the bottom."

"I can see how we wouldn't want that happening," Dearbhla remarked dryly.

"Well, then, folks," Landon said, giving the brim of his hat a little tug. "Let's get to it. We don't have all day."

There were already deep grooves in the earth where previous pioneers had navigated the steep descent. They formed three wide pathways that wound down at an angle across the hillside to the level ground below. Clyde felt grateful for those who had gone before, and made it easier for others to find a route that already had boulders and bushes cleared out of the way. Still, it proved to be no easy feat.

Sweat beaded the men's foreheads and glistened on their bare forearms. Wagons creaked and ground their way down the hill, sometimes keeling over dangerously to one side as their iron wheels grated on the rocks and gouged into the earth.

Shouts of "Hoooold 'er back!" and "Steady! Steadeeeee!" filled the air together with the dust swirling about both men and beasts. The mules were the most difficult. Most of them wanted to go careening down the hillside with no regard for the wagon behind them. More than once, a gentleman aired his lungs in the hearing of the ladies, and profuse apologies immediately followed.

One team of mules proved especially difficult. It was a team that belonged to a young black-haired man and his somber young wife. They had a little boy of about three who stared silently at everything going on around him, his eyes wide and a little frightened. Clyde considered that he had never heard the boy speak a word during the entire trip, but his mind was on other things, and he quickly thrust that thought aside.

"Maybe we should unhitch them, Mr. Morland," the young man suggested, his brow furrowed with consternation when his mules refused to move a step forward. "I'm afraid if we get them going, they'll take off like rabid dogs. They seem to have only two speeds. Too fast and dead stop."

"We could unhitch 'em and take the wagon down ourselves," Landon speculated, "if we had enough men with their strength to keep that wagon o' yours from draggin' us all down to the bottom in a heap."

One corner of the young man's mouth curled upward in a droll smile. "Sounds like something I'd rather avoid," he remarked.

"How about we hobble 'em, Pa?" Brady suggested, tucking his thumbs into his braces. "We could make the rawhide loose enough so they'll not feel off kilter, but tight enough so they don't get into their heads to start runnin'."

Landon nodded slowly. "We could try it," he agreed cautiously.

The plan worked until they were halfway down the hill. With little goat like jumps, the mules worked their way down the hill, the men ready on either side, some to steady the wagon, others heaving back on the ropes and chains that kept the wheels stationary. Inch by slow inch, they approached the base, and then the mules decided they had had enough. With a squeal of frustration, one of them reared up, snapping the hobbles around its front pasterns. The other followed suit and then aimed a vicious kick at the wagon behind it.

"Whoa! Whoa!" their owner cried out, trying to grab at the nearest mule's bridle.

"Get out o' the way, man! You'll get yourself killed!" Landon yelled, bodily launching himself at the fellow and wrenching him out of the way just as a pair of flailing hooves came crashing down where his skull had been only a hair's breadth of a second earlier.

The man hit the earth, groaning, as his mules sped off down the rest of the hill, the wagon bouncing and rattling dangerously over the last stretch. When they reached the other wagons, they slowed and stopped, dropping their heads to the grass and grazing as if nothing had happened.

"'Mules are stronger,' they said. 'Mules are faster,'" the hapless owner muttered all the way down the hillside, picking up miscellaneous items that had been thrown from his wagon in the mules' headlong stampede. "I wish I'd listened to the old man and bought oxen instead of these two widow-makers."

"Why don't you and your family camp with us tonight?" Clyde offered, feeling sorry for the stranger as he walked alongside him and helped to retrieve the scattered contents of his wagon. He knew how it felt to be completely out of one's depth. He was feeling it all the time lately. "I'll take a look-see what we can do about your wagon while the women fix supper."

"Well, that's right generous of you, mister, ah…"

"Henderson," Clyde introduced himself. "But you can call me Clyde."

"Slade," came the grateful response, "Connor Slade. I'll reimburse you for your labor, of course."

"Whatever you can manage." Clyde waved off the offer of payment. "Maybe somewhere along the trail you can roll a boulder out of my path."

"I've a feeling that could end up being more literal than figurative," Connor replied with a twinkle in his eye, despite his obvious fatigue and dispiritedness.

Clyde smiled.

They drew the wagons into a circle at Landon's command, even though it was not quite five o'clock yet. "We've all had a tough few days," he explained.

The weary pioneers were happy to oblige, and they retired to their wagons.

Clyde made good on his promise, and with Tess working as his eager assistant, he surveyed the damage to the Slades' wagon. "Not much structural damage, thank heavens," he said, wiping his hand off on his leather apron. "Tess and I will have this fixed before dark, I'm sure of it."

"Vie, tank you so much, Mr. Henderson," a young woman said as she came to stand beside Connor, her little boy hiding behind her skirts with his thumb in his mouth, his wide black eyes staring out at the world.

"You're so welcome," Clyde assured her, having no trouble deciphering the thick accent. "You must be Connor's wife."

"She sure *is* my wife, Clyde," Connor confirmed happily. "Her name is Gyorgyike, and this is our son, Gabor."

"Georgika and Gahbor," Clyde repeated slowly. "You're from Hungary, Mrs. Slade?"

"I am," the lady replied, looking taken aback that he had recognized her accent but apparently not wanting to appear too impressed. "Most people think I am from Germany, but they don't ask before they rattle away in German to me." Many of her th's sounded more like d's, and the w's were pronounced as v's.

"May I call you Gyorgyike?" Anna's voice chimed in as she appeared at her husband's side.

"Yes, yes, that is fine," the young woman agreed. "If you are needing help wit' the cooking, I am more than willing to help."

The women bustled away, and Clyde went to work on the wagon. Connor himself proved to be as helpful an assistant as Tess was, even though he needed everything explained to him. Thankfully, Tess did most of the explaining, leaving her father to focus on his work. Meanwhile, he found out a little about the Slades.

"This ain't just a trip for me, you know?" Connor started sharing of his own volition. "My grandfather, God rest his soul, was a soldier in the British army in 1779. Came to fight the Revolutionaries to take the colony of America back for the Crown. Except he turned when he saw how fiercely these men fought for freedom, or that's what he always told me."

"I suppose there's no reason to doubt him," Clyde remarked, hammering a nail into a plank of wood he was replacing on the wagon's front board.

"No, I don't suppose there is," Connor responded with a smile. "He also said it was a miracle they didn't find him and shoot him for desertion, but a Swiss woman who owned a bakery in Boston hid him in her shop and smuggled him off to Philadelphia. He came back soon as he could after the war was over and married her."

"So your grandmother's Swiss, then," Clyde noted, checking for damage on the axle and the wheels. Everything seemed in order, just as he had suspected.

"Was," Connor corrected him. "They both died when I was a little boy. My pa married a Yugoslav woman he rescued from a slave camp. Me, I decided I would find a bride in the mail order section of the papers. First time I saw her picture, I knew Gyorgyike was my wife."

"That's quite an interesting story," Clyde replied, nodding as he dusted off his hands and began to stow his tools away in the leather folder he always kept them in. "What brings you to the trail, though? It sounds like you had a good life in Boston."

"We did," Connor began, and then paused. "Well, I did. But I was bored, you know? Then I heard about Oregon, and I decided, what the hell, may as well go give it a gander. But I didn't want to go alone, you know? So I answered a mail-order bride advertisement, and here we are."

He spread his arms wide and laughed. Clyde nodded in understanding and asked no more questions.

That night, in their tent, he whispered to Anna. "I think those young Slades need a couple of good friends. You think we've got room for them in our already overstocked life?"

He felt his wife kiss him on the cheek and then snuggle closer against him. "You always were such a good man, Clyde Henderson," she said, her voice glowing with fondness and pride. "Of course we'll take the Slades under our wing. They're going to need all the friends they can get."

A moment of silence lapsed between them, and then Anna added, "I feel as if Gyorgyike isn't telling me everything."

"I thought the same thing about Connor," Clyde concurred.

"The strangest is their little boy. He hasn't said a word since the moment he first looked at me," Anna went on. "Even Billy couldn't get him to say anything, and you know how he gets quiet children out of their shells."

"I noticed that, too," Clyde replied, feeling sleep tugging at his eyelids. He quickly gave up the struggle and let them flutter closed, thankful their wagon train had not suffered worse damage on the steep hill that afternoon. As he drifted off to sleep, he wondered what the new day would bring them.

***

As darkness descended, the stars came out, first one by one, twinkling in the darkening sky, and then seeming to fill the expanse of the heavens with a mass of shimmering silver pinpricks as the sky turned to a thick, inky black. There was no moon to pale their brilliant light, nor to cast a shadow or illuminate a movement on the prairie.

A hastening, round-shouldered form, followed by a bigger, four-legged one, passed from one bush to another on top of the steep hill towering above the circled wagons that had made their slow and painful way down that very day. Two more forms followed the first one in the same way, and they conversed in whispers behind the concealment of the leaves.

"Looks like they're a hardy bunch, Carl," one of them rasped. "That feller leadin' 'em sure knows what he's about. He weren't hatched under a turkey, that's for sure."

"You gettin' cold feet, Amos?" the biggest of them growled.

"Naw, no chance," came the hasty reply. "Jus' thinkin' they'll be trickier to fool with him around."

"I been watchin' that other feller, the one that's always with 'im," a third voice with a slight whine to it said softly. "He's fresh from the city, no doubt about it."

"I ain't so sure, Max," Amos replied hoarsely. "From where I sit, he looked pretty handy with fixin' them wagons."

"They got carpenters in the city, too," Carl chipped in condescendingly. "How d'you think they get houses built and carriages made, eh?"

"Harrumph," Amos replied grumpily.

"I reckon Max is barkin' up the right tree, if I ain't mistook," Carl said thoughtfully. "That carpenter feller looks like he's the weak link in the chain, right there."

"So are we goin' in tomorrow or what? Ain't we been tailin' 'em long enough now?" Max lamented.

"Sure, we are," Carl replied, slapping him on the back. "But watch you do what I tell ya, y'hear? Don't try anything too soon. We got t' get 'em eatin' out of our hands first."

"I read ya, boss," Amos assured him, and Max grunted his assent.

"Good. Now, try t' get some shut-eye. We need our wits about us, sharper than they've ever been."

Carl followed his own advice, slumping down against a rock and pulling his hat down over his face. The other two followed suit, their horses grazing quietly on the grasses nearby. Carl's stomach grumbled. He was looking forward to a hot meal. It would be his first in days.

Chapter 9
Carl Cheatham

"Ahoy, the camp!" a voice rang out in the deathly silence that always preceded the first stirrings of nature anticipating the sun's coming rays.

Clyde raised himself up onto one elbow. The darkness was so thick he felt as if he could reach out and grab a fistful.

"Ahoy, the camp!" the voice cried again.

So he hadn't imagined it.

"Who is it? What do you want?" Norman's voice called out. He was once again on night watch but had evidently learned his lesson and not fallen asleep this time.

Clyde sat up and pulled on his coat and boots before sticking his head out between the front flaps of the tent. He looked about, wondering if it would even help to light a lantern. More likely, it would only make him an easy target to fire at. *Why would anyone approach a camp at this time of the morning, when there's no chance anyone can see them to tell whether they're friend or foe,* he thought. *Well, they called out. I'm sure a thief or a robber wouldn't do that.*

"We're needin' help," the voice called out again. "Three of us got robbed. Varmint took both our pack mules and all our supplies."

Clyde grabbed his rifle and stepped outside. A shadow moving in the darkness ahead of him told him Landon was just emerging from his own tent, his rifle also gripped in his hand. The coals in the campfire in the middle of the camp still glowed, but they gave no substantial light.

"Where are you?" Landon called out.

"Up on the hill," came the reply.

Both men looked up toward the sound, and Clyde saw a huddle of shadows moving down the treacherous hillside, only it seemed so much less life-threatening when there were no wagons involved, even in the darkness.

"It's all right, Norman," Landon called to the young man. "You stay at your post. We'll take it from here." He then whispered to Clyde, "We can't let them come into the camp until we've seen 'em face to face." He didn't need to explain why.

Clyde nodded, and together they went to meet the men outside of the circle of wagons.

"So sorry t' bother y'all at such an hour," the tallest of the men said as Clyde and Landon approached. He glanced back over his shoulder. "We figured we'd rather risk your rifles than run into the fellers who took our mules. Who knows what they might take this time around?" His voice was gravelly and husky, and filled with fear that sounded legitimate to Clyde.

"So you're lookin' for protection?" Landon cut right to the chase. It was clear he had erred on the side of caution and get down to the nitty-gritty regarding the motivations of the men approaching their camp.

"If you folks would be so kind," one of the other men replied, his voice a little whiny and scratchy. "Dang thieves took all our provisions, but we can hunt and make sure the camp has meat, if we could just travel with ya a little way."

"How far?" Landon demanded.

Clyde wondered if perhaps he wasn't being overcautious but reminded himself that Landon had produced a pretty consistent run of good decisions along the trail that had saved many of them a lot of trouble. He had not forgotten his call not to shoot at the Pawnees early after their departure from Independence.

"We're headed for California," the third man said in a gruff voice, and Clyde sensed Landon tensing up beside him.

"But for sure we'll manage fine if we can just get as far as Fort Laramie," the tall man cut in swiftly, a touch of irritation seeming to shade his tone. "Then we'll leave y'all in peace."

"Fort Laramie, eh?" Landon echoed, apparently stalling for time so he could think.

"Uh-huh," the whiny-voiced man confirmed.

"You fellers got names?" Landon enquired after another suspense-laden silence.

"Sure have," the tall man replied, seeming to perk up at the question. "Folks call me Carl. Carl Cheatham." He slapped the shoulder of the whiny man beside him. "And this here is Max Cooper. The other feller is Amos Feinstein."

"Landon Morland and Clyde Henderson. We're the leaders of the wagon train," Landon informed their visitors. The sky was lightening, and the dark shapes of men in front of them were taking more definitive shape. "Why don't ya come have a cup of Arbuckle's? I reckon our night watch should still have a can keeping warm on the coals." He stepped aside to let the men walk in front of them as they headed toward the camp. It struck Clyde that he was making sure they stayed in his sight for as long as possible before he made any move toward trusting them.

"Anything t' warm these frozen bones o' mine," Carl said as he took a step forward, and Landon suddenly held up his hand.

"If I get the teeniest whiff of any shenanigans, and I mean *any* kind of shenanigans, you're out on your ear. The lot of ya. Is that clear?" he said. His last phrase, although meant as a question, sounded more like a statement that the men were obliged to agree with. They did, and Landon let them walk by. He caught Clyde's eye in the mists of predawn and whispered, "Better grow eyes on the back of your head, Henderson. I got a hunch we're goin' t' be needin' 'em soon."

Clyde felt his shoulders tensing up. He fervently hoped Landon was being melodramatic, but he already knew him to be more inclined to make understatements than exaggerations.

"Norman," Landon addressed their night watchman. "You can get off early today."

"Thank you, kindly, Mr. Morland. Coals are still hot, and I made fresh coffee 'bout an hour ago, if y'all have a hankerin' for it. Should be enough to go around," the young man replied, bobbing his head in deference to the train leader, already retreating from the scene.

"Mighty decent of ya, Norman," Landon replied, touching the brim of his hat.

"You fellers had any trouble from savages yet?" Carl inquired in a blithe tone, as if making idle conversation while Clyde poured coffee into a tin mug produced from the backpack he was carrying.

Clyde opened his mouth to reply in the affirmative, but Landon cut him off before he could get a word out. "No, no trouble at all," he said, his face deadpan. "But that ain't surprisin' since we don't go givin' the *natives* any trouble." Landon gave Carl a pointed look.

"You sayin' we got our just deserts? Is that it?" Max whined, his eyes forming narrow slits that glinted in the first light of dawn breaking in the east.

"Just lettin' you know our policy, so you're on board with how we do things round here," Landon countered placidly. He took a sip of coffee and then continued, "I don't recall you fellers describing the varmint who took your mules."

"Oh, they were red men, all right," Amos grunted.

"I'm sorry t' hear that," Landon replied without missing a beat. "I've always said there's a bad apple in every bag, red, white, black, yellow. Tarnation, even God's chosen people had more than their fair share."

In the golden light of the rapidly rising sun, Clyde could see Carl carefully studying Landon. He could not pretend to know the sort of men who roamed the plains, but he had come across many in the city, and it was clear Carl Cheatham was a highly intelligent man. He obviously noticed things, but he knew when to keep quiet about what he saw and heard. Unlike his two companions.

The camp had been slowly coming to life while the men sized each other up on the outskirts where the cattle grazed.

Clyde could see Anna, Louise, Dearbhla, and Gyorgyike already at work getting breakfast ready, such as it was. Clyde thought back to breakfasts in Philadelphia. Fresh scones, cream cheese, jelly, preserves, fresh fruit, oatmeal, bacon that actually tasted like bacon. If he could have anything back from his old life, it would be those breakfasts.

"Why don't ya join us for some grub," Landon was saying. "We'll be hittin' the trail soon as we're done and cleaned up."

Carl and his companions nodded in assent, and Clyde joined them at the fire pit where the four families were in a bustle of preparation for the day and its first meal. Once introductions were completed, the men sat down and gratefully received plates full of food.

"You fellers off to Oregon, too?" Noel asked before taking a large bite out of his slice of pan bread.

"Nah, California," Amos drawled.

Noel's eyes lit up. "You're goin' to the gold diggings, then?"

"Sure," Carl said with a winning smile. Clyde had noticed he was far more friendly and relatable than the other two. "Me and the boys know some fellers down there who are already rakin' it in."

"Well, then they're the lucky ones," Landon commented, swallowing a mouthful of bacon and scrambled egg.

"Lucky? Hell, there's so much gold in them hills, folks are hittin' pay-dirt like nobody's business. It ain't luck, it's the lode!" Carl shot back, looking around at his audience to judge their reactions. The smile on his face didn't fade at the less than enthusiastic response from everyone but Noel.

"Yeah, and the ones who don't hit that lode, well they're just plumb out o' luck, is all," Amos added with a chuckle. They were evidently enjoying their little play on words.

"Sure sounds like it beats breakin' your back on a ranch to get crops out o' the ground and calves out o' the cows," Noel commented, his eyes becoming dreamy.

"I still think breaking yer back is the most honest, surest way. My pa always said, 'A bird in the hand is worth two in the bush,' and I'm inclined t' think he was right," Landon commented, casually picking his teeth as if he found the conversation slightly boring. "What's your take, Clyde?"

"Oh, I've been a tradesman all my life. I don't think I'd even know where to dig for gold. I can't speak for other folks, but I'd rather stick with what I know." Clyde tried to play it neutral without sitting too heavily on the fence. The look Landon gave him told him he approved and that his regard for and trust in Clyde had just gone up a notch or two.

"One man's meat is another man's poison, I reckon," Carl quipped, the smile on his face giving no clue whether or not he felt insulted. In fact, quite the opposite seemed true of him. Nothing seemed to faze him or his easygoing disposition.

Clyde wondered if his initial suspicion of the men had been nothing but a byproduct of being in an environment in which he felt more vulnerable than he could ever remember being before.

With the wagon train back on the trail again, the iron wheels adding their own bit of wear to the already deeply cut wagon tracks, Clyde and Landon walked alongside the lead wagon, accompanied by Carl and his friends.

"You know, since y'all have been such friendly hosts and all, we figured we'd waste no time and get to huntin' right away. Maybe we could even go down to the ol' Platte and see if we can catch some fresh fish. Max is a deft hand at things like that," Carl suggested as he strode alongside them with his easy, loping gait.

"You'll need horses, though, won't ya?" Landon noted, not changing expression in the least.

"That'll be a great help," Carl returned with what seemed to be genuine deference. "But we'll understand if you feel you'd rather give us time t' prove ourselves. Man in your position shouldn't be expected to trust three total strangers he only just met."

"You'd be right about that," Landon agreed, his eyes riveted on the wagon ahead.

For a moment, all of them walked on in silence.

Then Clyde spoke softly to Landon. "I've always seen the best way to win folks over is to trust them. That's when they prove themselves," he whispered. "If these three feel like we don't trust them, they won't feel any need to prove otherwise."

Landon gave him a sharp but thoughtful look. "I don't have a good feelin' about this," he said.

Clyde shrugged. "We'll be wanting folks to trust us one day," he whispered and then looked back at the trail.

Landon took a deep breath and nodded at their new acquaintances. "All right. See if there's a spare horse or three. But you'll return 'em by noon to their owners, without a scratch on 'em. Understood?"

"Sure thing," Carl agreed, his positivity still fully intact. He chucked his head toward the back of the wagon train. "I know who we can ask. Let's go," he said to Amos and Max as he jogged off in the direction he had indicated, motioning to them to follow.

Landon looked askance at Clyde. "I used to be like you, once," he remarked, his eyes serious. "Believed the best of every feller I set eyes on. But I paid a steep price for that trust. And like they say, once bitten, twice shy."

"I hope they don't prove me wrong," Clyde replied, feeling a little sheepish. He had a feeling Landon's suspicions might be well founded, but he could not bring himself to think ill of another human being, he did not even know well enough to distrust his motives.

They walked on in silence for a while, each immersed in his own thoughts, the warm morning sunshine beating on their backs. Clyde watched Nellie collecting wildflowers for her mother to paint. In the new, harsher terrain they were passing through, there were so many tiny flowers of vibrant and varied colors that seemed to bloom purely in defiance of the inhospitable landscape. The many bleached buffalo skeletons scattered about were a testament to the wild and fierce nature of their surroundings and had also provided much fodder for Anna's and Matt's sketchbooks.

Slowly, almost imperceptibly, the wide swathes of thick grass had thinned to clumps dotted between pale sands and loose sandstone rocks. Prickly pear and yucca had also become prolific, as well as a large variety of cactus plants that made for an interesting change in scenery but also posed new challenges of their own. He thought back to the punishment he had to lay on Billy for slipping a cactus pad onto the rock Matt had sat on at breakfast that morning. He would have to do something about Billy's penchant for mischief before he got up to something really serious.

Landon's iron grip on his arm brought Clyde's wandering thoughts to an abrupt halt. "Don't look directly, but up on the ridge at our left, tell me if ya see somethin'. Don't move yer head, just yer eyes, easy like."

Clyde had to make use of a substantial amount of self-control not to whip his head in the direction Landon had described, but he managed it and scanned the ridge in question, as his trusted friend had instructed. At first, he saw nothing, then the tip of an eagle feather, and another broke the line of the horizon. Two foreheads and two pairs of eyes followed and then disappeared again.

"I see them," he said, intentionally looking in the other direction. "Two of them."

"Where there's two, there's likely to be more," Landon remarked. "I ain't takin' chances."

Higher swells now marked the prairie, some of which formed small mesas and buttes. Between these hills were ravines, small and large, formed by the rains that pelted the stony earth at regular intervals, as their particular party had experienced often since the first time they had lost a day due to rain. At first, they had seemed like a blessed break in the monotony of rolling waves of grass, but now Clyde understood their potential for concealing hidden dangers.

Landon had taken the lead oxen's reins and was pulling them around to the right, intent on forming a circle. Clyde marched back to his wagon to fetch his rifle, informing each settler family as he went, without looking at them directly, that they were to form a circle and bring in the cattle and horses to the center. Some grumbled, others picked up on the gravity of his instruction and quickly complied.

He had only just lifted his weapon from its place in the wagon box and called to Billy to get himself over to the wagon pronto when the whooping and yelling started. Clyde felt his palm go sweaty again, his heart seeming to beat in his throat.

Billy, who had been sauntering over, gave a little yelp and burst into a run, diving for the back of the wagon. "I'll get my gun, Pa!" he yelled as he disappeared from sight.

Matt was by his side in a flash, ready to help protect his mother and siblings. The wagons were circling but were not yet there before the Lakota began circling them, their high-pitched cries cutting through the already humid morning air. Clyde and Matt half crouched behind the wagon box as it rumbled along, the oxen jostling and tossing their heads in fright at the sudden commotion.

A loud thwack near his head made Clyde look up right into the shaft and feathers of an arrow that had embedded itself into the wooden frame of the wagon cover. Every inch of skin on Clyde's body immediately went cold and clammy, and his mouth felt like it was filled with sand. Behind him, Matt raised his rifle and fired at a painted horseman riding by, missing him completely.

So this is it, Clyde thought fearfully. *This time they're firing at us. Good Lord, help us.*

Chapter 10
Unjust Deserts

A nauseating, hollow feeling plagued Matt's gut as he held his eye to the sights of the rifle in his hands. He wasn't sure if he had missed the bare-chested warrior because of nerves or cowardice. The idea of killing a man was something he had spent no time pondering, partly because he had a gut feeling it was an inevitability if he wanted to protect his family. And his friends. He just didn't want to think about it before he absolutely had to.

These men looked different to the Pawnee, who had launched the mock attack early in their journey. They boasted thick, black locks that were braided or simply tied into two ponytails hanging down over their chests. They had either one or two feathers sticking straight up on the back of their heads, and they wore buckskin pants decorated with fringes and colored beads.

They looked taller than the Pawnees, their faces more elongated and angular, their powerful upper bodies decorated with less fearsome adornments, but just as lithe and muscular. They carried small leather shields, painted with diverse patterns and images, with quivers slung across their backs and feather-festooned spears held aloft or balanced across their upper thighs as they galloped by, shooting arrows into the camp.

There were fewer of them than there had been of the Pawnee, so their cries were not nearly as deafening. But they were shooting, and not a laugh nor a smile cracked their stony features. Matt followed them with his rifle sights as they passed, ducking each time one turned their gaze on him.

He fired a few more times, but wasn't sure if he had struck anyone. A cry off to his left told him someone had been hit, but he didn't dare take his eyes off those coming closer to his family's wagon, so he did not know if it was one of the enemy or one of his own that had suffered injury.

Suddenly, more screaming erupted from the hillsides. It sounded different, perhaps even more wild than the Lakotas' cries, and was accompanied by rapid gunfire. The circling band immediately turned tail and fled. Matt kept his rifle trained on their backs, taking no chances. Then he heard an oath escape Landon's lips from where he stood, crouched behind his own wagon's protective bulk.

"Bejeebers!" he exclaimed. "It's Carl and his stooges firin' like a bunch of shannies. Better mind or they'll hit one of our folks."

In that moment, the three newcomers thundered past on their borrowed horses, still firing, whooping, and hollering at the tops of their voices. The attackers disappeared over a ridge in a cloud of dust, and the three men who had chased them off drew rein at the top of the rise, hurling dire threats after them. Matt wondered if the fleeing attackers could even understand those threats.

The three men rode back to the camp to an ecstatic welcome from most of the wagon train members. Only then did Matt notice the fish hanging from the leather thongs attached to their saddles. They had bunched them together by running a thin rope through each fish's lower jaw and tying a knot to keep it separate. Now they began cutting the black, shiny fish loose and handing them out to the excited crowd.

"Looks like they proved themselves today." Matt heard his father's voice at his elbow.

Noel and Connor stepped closer, each bearing two large carp in their hands.

"They sure did," Noel agreed enthusiastically. "And it looks like it's fish for lunch today, too. Here, this is your fair share. Sure will make an agreeable change from bacon-flavored salt." He grinned, holding out one of the fish to Landon.

The wagon train leader took the offering, but his face remained grave and pensive. "I ain't so sure Carl and his gang have proved anything, fellers," he said in a low tone that made Matt instinctively tighten his grip on the rifle in his hands. "Those were Lakota Sioux. All of 'em young fellers. There was no war chief with 'em, and they were shootin' like women. Whatever's cookin' here, it ain't smellin' fresh to me."

"Well, they chased them off," Clyde reminded him.

"Yeah, and they were far too obliged t' skedaddle. That's not how I know Sioux," Landon insisted thoughtfully, tugging at his mustache.

Connor shrugged. "All I know is they aren't bothering us anymore, and we got fish. Suppose we noon a little earlier? It's almost midday anyhow."

Landon cast a glance at the sun and nodded, his eyes still narrow slits of puzzled contemplation. The other two men slapped each other on the back and went to call their womenfolk. Soon the four families were gathered together to prepare the noon meal, the women urging the younger children to stay in the wagon for fear their attackers might return.

Matt took a plate of food over to Billy at his mother's request.

"I took a shot at one of 'em, Matt," his little brother whispered excitedly, waving his revolver in the air.

"I'm sure you did, Billy," Matt replied, taking the gun from his grip and stowing it in the box with the other firearms after he handed Billy his food.

"Do you think they'll come back?" Billy asked, taking a piece of fish and shoving it in his mouth.

"I guess nobody really knows," Matt replied. "Mr. Morland doesn't look happy with how things went. He reckons there's something not quite right about it all."

"I thought it was capital!" Billy enthused, his mouth full of fish and cornbread. "Did you see how Carl and his men chased 'em off? Bam! Bam! Bam!" He waved his iron spoon in the air, pretending it was a gun.

"Mr. Morland says they're Sioux. From what I've heard, those are the fiercest Indians out here. I feel like it's a little strange they gave up so quick. And we only had one injury.

Old Mr. Southey got an arrow in the arm. Mama's over there now, looking at his wound."

Billy's eyes widened. "You think Carl and the others were in on it? Maybe they're outlaws, with a bounty on their heads! Maybe we should catch 'em and turn 'em in at the next fort. We'll be heroes!"

"That'll be enough of that idle talk, now, William Clyde," their mother's voice interrupted their conversation, and Billy snapped his mouth shut. "You know what I've taught you about judging others. Don't forget, we'll have to answer to God himself for every idle word we speak, one day." She stowed her first aid box away in its place under the front seat of the wagon.

"I know, Mama," Billy said meekly. "I guess I'm just lookin' for some excitement is all."

"And you're talking just like a hillbilly, lately, too. Please tell me all the English lessons I've spent hours teaching you aren't being wasted," Anna responded, squeezing his shoulder playfully.

Billy's longing for excitement was soon satisfied again, though Matt wished they could have left it unslaked. He was walking alongside Butch and Bacon when the voices of Landon and Carl Cheatham reached his ears.

"Howdy, Mr. Morland," Carl greeted him expansively. "We were wonderin' how you enjoyed your fish dinner today. That ol' Platte might be too thin to plough and too thick to drink, but it sure breeds some mighty fine carp."

"It was mighty fine, thank you, Carl," Landon agreed, his voice civil but guarded.

"Pretty close shave we had with them savages back there," Carl went on happily. "I reckon me and the boys came back from our fishin' trip in the nick of time, eh?" He chuckled.

"I guess you could say so," Landon said noncommittally.

"Well, since you folks are lettin' us ride with ya and givin' us safety in numbers, we figured it wouldn't be a bad idea for us t' help y'all fight off the Indians. This here's Sioux country, but I reckon you know that already. Might be a good idea to have men on the lookout round the clock. We'd be more than happy to do that for y'all, since y'all have been so kind and welcoming to us."

Matt thought he detected a shadow of cynicism in Carl's voice as he concluded his offer. He listened carefully for Landon's reply, which, as was usually the case, was a few moments in coming.

"I'm sure we'd all be mighty grateful to ya, Carl," he accepted, his tone of voice still evincing the fact he did not intend to become bosom buddies with the newcomer anytime soon. "We'll keep our own on night watch duty, though. Like you said, safety in numbers."

"Well, I'm sure glad we see eye to eye, Mr. Morland," Carl said, and that was the last Matt heard of the conversation. His eyes strayed to the Morland wagon ahead of him, where Carrie and his sister Nellie were walking together and clearly having an animated conversation. Even from that relative distance, Matt could make out the soft hues of Carrie's flaxen hair, the now golden tan of her skin where the three-quarter sleeves of her dress left the lower part of her forearm exposed to the sun.

"Howdy, Matt!"

Brady's voice sounded beside him, making him jump as his cheeks grew hot at being caught red-handed ogling Carrie. He knew it was silly, as Brady could hardly read his mind. Still, he felt like a fraud. He would have to do something about it soon. He would have to tell someone, though he balked at sharing those kinds of things with his tough, manly new friend.

"I figured I'd give you a warning," Brady went on without waiting for a return greeting from Matt. "Mrs. Grant is missing a pearl necklace she inherited from her mother, with matching earrings, she says. She's gone and decided that Billy is the most likely to be the thief."

Matt whipped his head round to stare at Brady in disbelief. "Now look here," he said, his cheeks flushing for entirely a different reason than before. "I know Billy can get up to mischief now and then, but he's no thief. Ma would skin him alive if he so much as stole a feather off one of Mrs. Grant's chickens, and he knows it."

Matt remembered the pain of the cactus spines piercing the skin of his posterior, but that only strengthened his resolve to defend his brother. As much as he had often contemplated dragging young Billy over his knee to give him an almighty whupping, he could not imagine his little brother stooping so low as to steal. Especially such valuables. Now that he thought of it, Mr. Hopkins had also mentioned that his new gold watch was missing, and Greg, the man who had inherited George Barker's wagon when he absconded, was missing a Spanish saddle.

"Hey, don't shoot the messenger," Brady shrugged. "I'm only tellin' ya what Mrs. Grant said."

Matt felt immediate regret. "I'm sorry, Brady," he apologized quickly. "I'm feeling really jumpy, and I do not know why."

"There sure is somethin' stirrin' in the camp," Brady agreed. "Never you mind, though. We're more than a match for whatever it is."

Matt wished he could share Brady's certainty. Not only because he wanted things to be okay in the camp, but because he worried how a confident young woman like Carrie, with a brother and father like Brady and Mr. Morland, would even notice a pale, quiet boy like himself, full of self-doubt and insecurities. If he couldn't even approach her for a simple conversation, how was he going to handle any kind of unrest in the camp?

That evening around the fire, with his father playing the fiddle and Noel strumming along on his banjo, Matt stared alternately at the fire and at Carrie, trying to think of some excuse to go over and talk to her. She and Nellie seemed to be hitting it off, and he was about to give it up as a poor job, when Norman sauntered over and appeared to invite Nellie for a walk.

His sister blushed and jumped up, turned to say something to Carrie, and then tripped lightly away from the huddle of people, her hand on Norman's arm. Her father called something after her, but Matt didn't hear what it was. His entire focus was taken up with Carrie, now sitting alone, the firelight dancing on her smooth skin and gleaming braids. He stood slowly and uncertainly to his feet. As he reached his full height, she looked up, and their eyes locked. Matt took one step forward, and then a movement by her side made him stop.

It was Carl Cheatham, all white-toothed smiles and lithe, languid limbs filling up the space Nellie had previously occupied, arresting Carrie's attention. Matt cursed himself inwardly for being so slow as he sank down incrementally to his seat, a small wooden stool he first quickly checked for any cacti. As he sat down, feeling despondent and resigned, Carl caught his gaze. His eyes were dark and glittering and sent a chill down Matt's spine.

For all his smiles and apparent heroism, there was something about the man that was making Matt think maybe Mr. Morland had a point about not trusting him much too soon. He broke eye contact and stared into the flames, forgetting what Mr. Morland had said about not staring into the fire and giving himself night blindness. In that moment, he would have preferred to be blind, anyway, even if he had thought about it.

Eventually all the settlers retired to their respective wagons and tents, with Carl, Max and Amos taking up their new positions as watchmen. Matt had the first watch guarding the cattle and horses, and the man who would take over from him at midnight was a quiet, black-bearded man named Henry who Matt knew little about, other than he was humble but solidly dependable.

Matt's sleep that night, after his uneventful sentry shift, was fitful and filled with dreams in which he kept walking after Carrie, trying to catch up to her. No matter how fast he ran or how hard he climbed, the space between them kept growing wider and wider until she was nothing but a little golden speck in the distance. He woke, sweating, even though the earth had cooled during the night. He lay still, listening to the night sounds of the surrounding prairie, and then he realized there was a faint droning that reminded him of distant thunder.

He listened, trying to find out where it was coming from, and then realized it was a continuous rumble that was slowly and steadily fading away. He sat up, trying to imagine what it might be, but nothing came to mind. He rolled over, intending to sleep again, but his eyes refused to shut and ended up staring at the dying embers of the fire in the middle of the wagon circle.

A groan and a mutter alerted his attention as the cold dew settled on the stones and grass all around the wagon. Matt crawled out from under the prairie schooner and peered into the gray mist that hung around the camp. The groan sounded again, and he moved toward the sound that seemed to come from the other side of the circle of wagons. A dark form came into view, lying sprawled on the ground. Another groan rose in the cool morning air, and this time Matt knew it was coming from the man in front of him.

Quickly, he stooped to the man's side and tugged at his shoulder, rolling him over onto his back. The hair above his temple was matted and caked with blood. His eyes were glazed behind his drooping, fluttering eyelids. He groaned again.

"Pa!" Matt yelled. "Mr. Morland! Something's happened to Henry!" He stood up and began trying to probe through the mist swirling around him. If their sentry had been incapacitated, that could mean only one thing. Stepping over the motionless but still intermittently groaning form of Henry, he moved in the direction of the makeshift holding pens they had set up for the animals. The cattle were still there, but not a horse in sight.

"The horses! Has anyone seen the horses?" Matt yelled, his stomach contracting into a knot. Even George Barker's Clydesdales were gone. He stumbled back to where Henry lay. His mother, shrouded in his father's coat, was already inspecting the hapless man's head wound.

As the day broke full of birdsong and a glorious sunrise, it was completely lost on the wagon train travelers. Without horses, their journey would be even more difficult than it needed to be.

Landon was already checking the ground for a trail. "Sioux," he said grimly. "They don't hardly leave a trail, but there's barefoot ponies' hoof marks that you can't miss if you know what to look for."

"And I suppose there's no way we can go after them," Clyde stated rather than asked, "since we have no horses."

"You ain't wrong," Landon confirmed.

Matt felt an anger rising in his chest that he had never felt before. Everything was so unfair. They were all just trying their best to carve out a better life for themselves and their families, and everything seemed to conspire against them. Especially since those men, Carl and his friends, had come into their little world. He stopped in the middle of his thought. "Anybody seen Carl?" he asked, looking around.

He caught his father's eye, and understanding dawned brighter than the sun that had just begun poking its blinding rays over the eastern horizon.

"No," Clyde and Landon said in humorless unison.

"And Max and Amos neither," Landon added, his voice as gravelly as his eyes were stony.

"They took our horses? After all we did for them?" Matt spluttered in disbelief.

"If you ask me, that was Carl's plan from the beginning," Landon remarked, folding his arms over his broad chest as he peered off into the direction the stolen animals' hoof marks led. "Ladies and gents, I reckon we've been had."

Chapter 11
Metamorphosis

Spirits were low as the overlanders prepared their breakfast and readied their teams of mules and oxen for the day's journey. Matt couldn't help noticing that even Helen was silent, too depressed to complain about anything. There would be no climbing on a horse's back for anyone who got tired, and Landon had warned his traveling companions to ride in their wagons as little as possible.

"We ain't on level ground anymore," he elaborated at the predeparture meeting held with all the menfolk. "Draggin' those wagons uphill and brakin' 'em down dale, well, that's enough to make any ox plumb wore out at the end of the day. Let's not make it worse for 'em. Folks have killed oxen and mules just by pure overwork."

It was a solemn admonition. Nobody needed to be told the loss of an ox or mule would make life exponentially more difficult when they got to the famed South Pass in the Rockies and the Blue Mountains beyond that.

"And one more thing," Landon added just before the huddle of men scattered to their respective wagons. "Keep your eyes peeled and your shootin' irons handy, fellers. I'll wager we ain't seen the last of Carl Cheatham, or whatever his real name is."

The men nodded, their countenances dour.

Henry, his head covered in fresh but crude bandages, spoke up. "I reckon we know who's been stealin' from us, now. I heard some of y'all figured it was young Billy, but I'll wager my last dime it was Cheatham and his lowlife no-accounts."

Matt heaved a sigh of relief as all the men nodded in unison, grunting their agreement.

"And I'll wager mine they'll be back for more," Landon added. Another chorus of nods and grunts followed his words. "Well, let's head out, fellers," he concluded before he abruptly spun on his heel and headed for his waiting wagon.

They had scarcely gone two miles when Matt saw them. Silhouetted against the bright morning sky, Carl and his gang sat on their stolen horses high on a ridge and watched the train passing by. Matt tried to pretend he hadn't noticed them, but he called out to Brady, who was leading his father's oxen. "You see what I see up on the ridge, Brady?"

"Oh, I see 'em. I'm itchin' for 'em to come down here and let us give 'em a whippin' like they ain't ever had in all their born days!"

Matt wished again he had been blessed with just a smattering of Brady's confidence and bravery. If he was honest, the sight of the wily outlaws atop the ridge made his stomach turn with fear. Suddenly, he heard the grass rustling behind him, and the next moment, Carrie and Nellie were on either side of him.

"Can we walk with you, Matt?" Nellie asked.

"Sure," he replied, squirming a little. He could already feel his tongue tying itself into knots. "You see those varmints up on the ridge?" he added, trying to emulate Brady's confident tone but painfully aware his speech sounded contrived and unnatural.

"That's why we'd rather walk with you," Carrie informed him, linking her arm through his. Matt felt a thousand little pins and needles stabbing at his skin as his stomach did a flip-flop. He could almost feel Carl's eyes boring into him from his elevated and distant vantage point.

"I reckon you'd be safer with your Pa and Brady," he mumbled, every nerve in his body focused on the warmth of her slim, soft arm radiating through the woolen sleeve of his shirt.

"Those two would more likely run after the danger and leave me behind than stay and protect me," she retorted with a tinkling laugh.

"Ha ha" was all Matt could manage. He sneaked a peek up at where Carl had last stood and saw the three men had disappeared. His throat felt dry. What more did they want from them? Wasn't it enough they had taken the most valuable of their possessions? Why could they not leave them at peace? An angry frustration rose in his chest.

"Nellie tells me she hardly knows her brother anymore," Carrie remarked nonchalantly. "Do you like living on the wild prairie better than the city now?"

Matt stalled for a moment, not sure how to interpret Carrie's line of questioning. "Well, I've never fired a gun before I came on this trip," he hedged. "Can't say I like it too much, but if needs must, a man's got to do what a man's got to do."

"You sound just like my pa, now," Carrie interjected, a smile clear in her voice even though her bonnet hid her features from his view.

Matt felt himself redden. "I'm not sure I'll ever measure up to your pa, Carrie," he protested mildly. "He's the real dyed-in-the-wool cowboy type. He's smarter than most folks I know, and he doesn't know the meaning of fear."

At that moment, a cry went up from the back of the wagon train, and two shots cracked like whips in the morning air. Brady spun around and held out the oxen's lead rope to his sister. "Carrie! Hold on to these fellers while I go help Pa!" he yelled, hardly giving her time to run forward and grab the lariat before he dashed away up the line of wagons.

"You see what I mean?" Carrie asked laughingly, watching her brother's feverish departure.

Matt nodded, giving her a wry grin.

"Please stay with us and Ma, Matt?" Nellie entreated him nervously. He patted her hand, which he now realized was hooked through his other arm. His attention had been so taken up with Carrie's presence he had hardly noticed it.

"Don't worry, I ain't going anywhere," Matt assured her warmly. What he could do to keep her safe, he had no real idea. His hand strayed to the revolver in his pocket that Landon had given him. The rifle he had shouldered had done nothing but make a loud noise at their last altercation. He was not sure the revolver would do much else.

There were more cries and shots from the rear of the wagon train, and then all grew silent again.

Soon Brady came trotting up to them and took over from his sister once more. "Lazy prairie dogs took Mr. Hopkins's chicken coop off the end of his wagon," he informed the trio. I think we might have nicked one of 'em, but Mr. Hopkins noticed 'em too late to get a good sight on 'em."

It was not the last incident. For the next few days, the outlaws struck at irregular times and in various places along the line of wagons. Sometimes they merely frightened the emigrants, and sometimes they snatched something from a wagon. One night, they got a whole keg of gunpowder out of Greg's wagon.

By the fourth day, everybody's nerves were frayed. The frequent afternoon thunderstorms that had become as much a refreshment as they were a frustration were now viewed with a sense of fear. Carl and his gang liked to work under cover of the rain, it seemed.

After a morning of tense but uneventful travel, Landon called noon, and the wagons rumbled around into their usual circle shape. Almost automatically it seemed to Matt. Casting their eyes about at the nearby ridges and intently examining every movement or rustle of leaves or grass, the emigrants set about preparing the noon meal. Nobody went off to look for a little game meat to shoot. Nobody wanted to run into Carl and end up in a skirmish that could only end badly.

Hardly tasting his chunk of pot bread and the unvarying bacon, Matt sat listening to Noel trying to make small talk with little success. The sound of a spur jingling caught his ear, and he sat up straight. It seemed to come from behind him. He looked up into Nellie's face and noted she had gone white as a sheet. She gripped her mother's hand on one side and Carrie's on the other as they all stared at whatever was behind him.

Slowly, Matt turned around as his father and Landon were doing the same. None other than Carl Cheatham stood there, picking his teeth with a stick while he grinned at them, his hat pushed back rakishly on his head of bushy light brown hair.

"Surprised to see me?" he quipped, lifting one boot and planting it on the nearest wagon tongue with a devil-may-care look on his face.

Landon's hand went straight to his revolver and hovered there as his eyes narrowed. "Surprised, no. But you'll be havin' yourself a surprise if you don't get those horses of ours back where they belong," he growled.

Carl wagged one finger in the air. "Now, you just hold your horses, mister," he said and then chuckled at his own joke. "Oh, wait, you ain't got none!" Then his face became sullen. "I'd keep my paws away from that firing iron if I were you. Max and Amos ain't too bright, but they sure know how t' shoot." He tossed his head at one wagon where some children were playing a game of tic-tac-toe in the sand. "We wouldn't want anybody to get hurt now, would we?"

The look in the outlaw's eyes sent an icy shiver down Matt's spine. He knew it was not an empty threat. He stepped back instinctively and folded his arms over his chest.

"What do you want, Cheatham?" Landon barked, his hand still hovering near his gun belt, though not as close as before.

"Well, now," Carl responded expansively, the insolent smile returning. "That's more like it. I thought you'd never ask." He pulled at his mustache, and his eyes roved immediately to where Carrie sat.

Matt's stomach turned at the glint of uncouth appreciation in those eyes, and a fire of protective rage smoldered in his belly.

"What I want," Carl went on, "is t' make a deal with ya, Mr. Morland. If you think you could stoop so low."

"Spit it out, Carl," Landon demanded, clearly nearing the end of his tether.

Carl seemed not to hear him. Instead, he walked to the middle of the circle and gave a low bow. "Mr. Morland," he said with mock deference. "If I could have your daughter Carrie's hand in marriage, I'd be the happiest man in the world. Then there'd be no reason for me and my men to hang around your camp anymore. I'll take her to the goldfields and treat her like a queen soon as I've made my fortune."

Matt stared at Landon. His normally deadpan face was pale and contorted with anger. But before Landon could respond, a woman's voice with a heavy accent cut into the breathless stillness.

"I have seen your kind of man, Cheatham. You will treat her like a whore, not a queen." It was Gyorgyike, her eyes flashing, her face set like granite. "You will have your way wit' her, and then you will make your fortune selling *her* as a saloon girl." She spat into the dirt at her feet.

Carl gave her a withering stare. "I wasn't talkin' to you, you Bavarian fruitcake." He sneered derisively and turned his attention back to Landon. His charming smile was back, but his eyes were shrewd and calculating.

"My daughter is not for sale, Mr. Cheatham," Landon said, his voice calm, his gaze unwavering. "And if you don't quit botherin' us, I'll send the cavalry after you as soon as we set foot in Fort Laramie."

Matt felt an even deeper appreciation stirring in his chest toward Landon.

"Now, now, Mr. Morland," Carl rebuffed him. "That's a pretty hasty decision that could cost all these honest folks around you more than they can afford right now. You never know when those savages might decide t' come callin' again."

Landon drew his revolver from its holster and pulled the hammer back. "If you don't cut dirt out of here right now, you filthy coyote, I'll put a bullet between your eyes. You hear me?"

Carl put up his hands. "I know, I know, it's kinda sudden. I'll give ya a couple days t' think it over. But my terms stay the same." As he spoke, he stepped out of the circle between Matt and Clyde and then back the way he had come between the wagons.

Matt watched Landon follow him, the revolver still pointed at his head, then his gaze shifted to Carrie. Her face was as white as a sheet, but she sat up straight, gripping her mother's hand on one side and Nellie's on the other. Her jaw was set squarely, and her eyes were fiery as she kept her gaze on her father. Matt got the feeling she was mad at Carl, more for threatening her family than for demanding her as a payment for leaving the wagon train unmolested.

The sound of hoofbeats dying away echoed out over the prairie as a few of the other settlers left their noon fires and came running over to the huddle of four families. A barrage of questions followed, and the men responded, Landon barking more orders for increased vigilance, not only over goods but over women and children. Matt could only sit quietly, staring at Carrie. She was going to need a real man to look after her, and he didn't know if he had what it took.

That night, as he lay under the wagon, not trying too hard to fall asleep, he heard his parents talking.

"Did you hear what Gyorgyike said?" Anna asked softly.

Her husband gave a grunt of affirmation.

"Something tells me there's more to that young woman's story than any of us know," Anna went on. "I think she's known more pain than she's even told Connor about."

"I'm sure she'll end up confessing all to you, my dear," Clyde replied, his voice warm with affection. "You draw troubled souls like bees to a honeycomb."

They fell silent after that, and Matt shifted position so he could see Carrie and Helen's tent. The whole day since Carl's visit, he had felt as if they were being watched. Carl had said he would give Landon a few days, but Carl had also proven they could not trust him to keep his word. He wondered if the outlaw was watching the white canvas covering that hid the young women from sight.

Deep into the night, Matt lay with his eyes riveted to the tent. Around him, they could hear the occasional murmurs and sounds of movement at greater and greater intervals until only the cicadas and the wolves disturbed the stillness of the night. Matt felt his eyelids growing heavy, but he fought valiantly against sleep. Whenever his eyes fell closed, he envisioned the unholy intent in Carl's eyes and shook himself awake again.

Suddenly, a noise alerted him. It sounded like the careful treading of feet on the rocky desert floor. Then a curt whisper. Matt realized his eyes were closed and he quickly opened them. He must have fallen asleep. For how long, he did not know. A footfall sounded close to his head. Another whisper sounded near the front of the wagon.

Matt glanced over at Carrie's tent. All seemed as it had been before. Then a shadow moved across the dirty white canvas, and another. At first Matt didn't register what was happening until he saw the glint of moonlight on the blade of a bowie knife as it came down in an arc and cut a long slash in the tent's roof with a soft zipping sound. "Hey!" he yelled, grabbing the rifle lying beside him and almost hitting his head on the wagon box in his haste to get on his knees and crawl out. "What are you doing?"

The only response was a flurry of movement and a muffled scream, and then a louder scream from the direction of the tent.

By the time Matt was on his feet, the two shadows were off and running. "Pa! Mr. Morland!" Matt sounded the alarm. "They've got Carrie!" He swung round, pointing his rifle at the figures disappearing into the night, but his finger hesitated on the trigger. He was no longer afraid of shooting a man. He was afraid that if he shot at those men, he might accidentally kill the woman he was trying to save.

"Don't shoot," Brady's voice said unnecessarily beside him.

"We have to go after them, Brady," Matt stated without thinking, as he lowered the rifle. "We have to get Carrie back safe." Brady looked at him. Although all he could see was the reflection of moonlight in his friend's eyes, he knew they were thinking the same thing.

"Pa! We're goin' after Carrie," Brady announced, without waiting for his father's consent. Gripping Matt's wrist, he stowed his Colt Paterson in his pants pocket. "Do whatever I tell ya, Matt. We'll show these sons of guns a thing or two."

Matt slung the rifle over his shoulder. He was about to move forward when a firm hand on his other shoulder stopped him. Glancing back into the face of Landon Morland, he prepared himself to defy an elder's orders, something he was not in the habit of doing. Instead, he felt Landon's other arm knock against his and looked down to see a fistful of lead balls glinting in the moonlight on top of a leather powder pouch.

"You'll need these, son," he said gruffly. "I know you want to prove yourself, and I ain't averse to givin' you the chance. Now, don't let them sidewinders lay a hand on my daughter."

Matt held out his hand for the shot and powder. As soon as they touched his palm, he shoved them into his pocket. Looking into the grinning face of Brady, he gave a single, decisive nod, and the two young men took off running, following the sound of receding hoofbeats.

With his feet pounding the earth and his heart pounding against his ribs, Matt knew he was leaving behind the boy who had fallen asleep under the wagon that night. He needed nobody to tell him that, whether or not he returned as Carrie's rescuer, he would never be the same again.

Chapter 12
Courthouse Rock

At first the tracks of the kidnappers' fleeing horses were easy to see in the bright moonlight, and the young men loped along at an easy jog. Brady pressed on at a constant pace for what felt like an hour at least without letting up. Matt felt himself tiring, but he pushed all thoughts of rest out of his mind as he dodged cacti and large rocks in his path, intent on the trail leading them onward. Carrie needed him now, and there was no way he was going to let her down while he still had the chance.

Brady stopped so abruptly that Matt almost ran into him. He held a finger to his lips and pointed ahead. The men had slowed their horses to a walk, apparently confident in the assumption that they had left any pursuers far behind. Now they were only a matter of yards ahead of the two young men. Brady dropped to the ground and pulled Matt down with him. They could just make out the luminescent whiteness of Carrie's nightdress stirring in the breeze.

One kidnapper held her in front of him as he sat astride his horse. She was giving her captors a hard time of it, and Matt almost wondered if she would need them to rescue her at all. It was a fleeting thought, though. He knew no amount of attitude or charm would persuade Carl to release his prize.

"Get your paws off me," her shrill, angry cry reached them on the still night air. The men laughed and paid her no heed. She kept struggling and protesting, but it was as if they were so accustomed to taking people against their will that her attempts to break free didn't even upset them. "My pa'll come for me and you'll all be sorry, just you wait," she warned them. One man said something, and they all laughed again.

Matt looked over at Brady.

"We got to play this thing smooth," Brady said in a hoarse whisper. "We ain't a match for all three of 'em awake. We might have t' trail 'em till they stop for a break and get some shuteye. Then we take our chance."

Matt nodded, thinking to himself that if Carl harmed even a hair on Carrie's head, he might not hold himself back from disregarding Brady's instructions.

They watched the riders disappear over the next rise, and Brady led the way up a shallow ravine that ran along it to the top. Carefully, they peered over. The men were still riding. The muffled sounds of Carrie still struggling to free herself from the grip of the man who held her captive drifted across to them. Judging by his height compared to the others, Matt concluded it must be Carl who held the hostage in his iron grasp.

The temptation was strong to shoot the man in the back, but Matt could not bring himself to lift the 1841 percussion rifle in his sweaty grasp to his shoulder. If he was going to kill someone, it would have to be in a more justifiable way.

Doggedly, he stuck to following closely on Brady's shoulder, mimicking his every move.

On and on they kept going for what felt like hours until Matt noticed the sky was lightening, but the men showed no sign of stopping. Carrie's protestations had become weaker and more widely spaced. She was clearly tiring, though it was clear her spirit remained strong.

At last, with the eastern sky turning dusty pink, Carl called for a halt. "May as well have breakfast, fellers," he said, sliding from his horse with Carrie still firmly in his grasp. "Amos, help me tie her up," he added, pinning Carrie's hands behind her back.

Matt tensed, ready to charge at them or fire a warning shot.

Brady placed a hand on Matt's shoulder. "Not yet," he whispered, and the two shrunk back behind the ravine they were using for cover.

Far in the distance, Matt could see the thin finger of Chimney Rock sticking up from the earth. Billy had spotted it two days before already and had worked all the children up into a frenzy, hedging bets on how many days it would take before they got there. Some of the youngest had driven their already tense parents nearly to distraction, asking a dozen times a day when the wagon train would reach Chimney Rock.

Right above their heads, where they crouched down behind a sandstone ridge, watching the movements of the kidnappers and Carrie, the imposing bulk of Courthouse Rock and the smaller Jailhouse Rock blotted out most of the sky. It would have been an impressive sight in less distracting circumstances.

As it was, the only reason Matt even noticed the two great monoliths was because Carl and his thugs had stopped between the sandstone buttes for their morning meal. Matt had to hand it to them: it was a smart move, since any smoke from a fire would be hidden by the large rock structures long enough to dissipate higher in the air and not attract attention from passing travelers.

As he watched the men preparing their breakfast, he chafed against the waiting. Maybe they should have brought more men with them, then they would have stormed Carl's camp by that time, and Carrie would already be safe. Then again, a flurry of shooting would only put Carrie in more danger. Besides, there was no telling what Carl had instructed his Sioux friends to do to the rest of the camp after he had gotten Carrie out. For all they knew, it was a trap to lure away the men of the camp and leave the women and children alone and unable to defend their wagons and their lives.

Amos shook out a bedroll and bedded himself down in a clump of winterfat shrubs and long grass. Matt felt his legs going numb and tried to stretch them out without making enough noise to alert the kidnappers to their presence. His throat was parched, and his stomach ached from hunger.

The smells of coffee drifting up from the fireplace only made things worse. But all he could think of was getting Carrie out of their clutches. Carl was trying to get her to eat something, but she refused, pulling her head away as far as it would go while she strained against the ropes that bound her hands and feet. Carl laughed and finished the meal himself.

Finally, the other man, Max, bedded himself down for a nap, too, but Carl kept watch, his eyes scanning the horizon that was still visible between the rock formations as he nursed the coffee in his tin cup. Brady gave a little cough and Matt looked at him.

"You cover me," Brady whispered. "I'm goin' down t' fetch my sister."

Matt stared at him blankly. "Cover you?" he repeated, without comprehension.

"Keep the end of that rifle pointed at Carl. If he shucks his shootin' iron, you pull the trigger," Brady explained.

Matt swallowed, doubts flooding his mind once more about whether he was the man for the job. But this was not the time to have doubts. He had to do what was necessary, and that was all there was to it. He nodded resolutely, gritting his teeth.

The two young rescuers had stationed themselves slightly above the kidnappers' campsite, partway up the lower slope of Courthouse Rock, and it was from this vantage point that Brady inched his way down toward Carl's campsite. When he was close enough to spring a surprise, he stood up straight with one hand in his pocket. Matt knew he was ready with his revolver.

"I'm here t' take my sister home," Brady growled in a low voice as he approached Carl from the back.

Carrie sprang unsteadily to her feet. "Brady?" she gasped.

Carl didn't even turn around. "You by yourself, boy?" he sneered. "Your daddy know you're here?"

"Yeah, he knows," Brady answered only the second question, leaving his adversary uncertain of the answer to the first.

Carl's grin faded as Brady slid his bowie knife from its sheath and calmly cut the ropes around Carrie's wrists without taking his eyes off Carl. Just as he handed her the knife to cut the bonds off her ankles, Max sprang up from his resting place, palming his revolver as he came erect.

Matt felt a shock course through his body as he swung the rifle's sights from Carl to the emerging form of Max. Without thinking, he lined up the sights and squeezed the trigger. The force of the shot shifted him bodily backward on the loose sandstone he lay upon. In the same instant, he saw Max's body jerk.

The kidnapper's gun hand stopped rising as he pulled off the shot too soon and sent the bullet thudding into the earth at Carrie's feet. A confused look crossed his face as he dropped the weapon and clutched at the patch of crimson forming on his shirt's left pocket.

As Max fell to his knees, Carrie cut frantically through the last of the rawhide thongs binding her ankles. Matt's fingers trembled as he tried to reload as quickly as possible. If only it wasn't such a long procedure, but he thanked Heaven for the rifle loading competitions Brady had challenged him to. Of course, his friend had always won, but Matt's fingers were no longer strangers to the task.

Carrie was screaming and cursing like a lady never should, and Matt looked up from reloading just in time to see Carl's fist plant an uppercut on Brady's jaw and send him hurtling to the ground. Brady had hardly hit dirt before Carl rushed

Carrie, grabbed her, and lifted her bodily up onto his shoulder. She beat and kicked at him, cursing and screaming all the while.

Max was now lying face down in the dirt, but Matt didn't have time to dwell on whether he had killed his first man. Amos was now also erect and pointing a revolver at Brady, who was scrambling back to his feet. Matt inhaled, as his friend had taught him, lined up the sights once more, and squeezed the trigger. He was ready for the mule kick this time and watched Amos drop his gun as he yelled out in pain and gripped his shoulder.

Quickly, Matt ducked down behind his cover of sandstone and grass and loaded again. His fingers seemed to work with no instructions from his brain, and within seconds, the gun was primed and ready to fire another shot. Amos was taking another lunge at Brady, who was scrambling up the side of the Courthouse Rock butte in hot pursuit of Carl and the still screaming Carrie.

Matt took careful aim and fired again, this time smashing the round lead ball into the outlaw's leg. He bellowed with pain and then seemed to decide they were outnumbered, so he had better save his skin while he had the chance.

Feeling detached and mildly surprised at his own calm state of mind, Matt loaded again, conscious that Brady was now free to pursue Carl and Carrie, but would definitely need help to bring the criminal down. He could hear the rapid tattoo of a retreating horse as the wounded Amos made his getaway, but Matt's focus was on Brady, in hot pursuit of the maddeningly tenacious kidnapper running off with his sister. He slung the rifle over his shoulder and climbed the sloping sides of the rock formation. There was no need for tracking anyone. Carrie's cries told him clearly where to go.

He caught up to Brady at the steepest part of the incline, where the smooth sandstone rock made it almost impossible to climb. There were two more steps on the butte up to its summit. "I think he's taken her round to the other side," Brady said in a low, earnest tone. "We'll have t' split up. You go left, I'll go right. Whatever ya do, don't shoot. If we hit Carrie…" He didn't finish his sentence.

Matt nodded in silent agreement, and both quickly moved off in their respective directions. The side Matt had been appointed was the more sloping side of the elongated butte. Scrambling along the spine of the rise, he noticed that Carrie's cries had become muted, as if Carl had gagged her or had his hand over her mouth.

Scrambling up to the summit, he followed the sound as quietly as he could and soon looked down on the level below him. He felt the weight of the rifle on his back and remembered Brady's warning not to shoot and stood undecided about what to do next. Then he realized with a shock that Carrie's cries had ceased and an eerie stillness settled all around them. Not even a bird called.

Matt paused, his heart beating in his throat. If that snake had killed Carrie, Matt knew he would not be in control of what he did next. A white flash of movement caught his eye, and he realized he was looking into a crevice in the rock at his feet. He took a step back and quietly shimmied down the side of the top sandstone layer of the butte. There was no sign of Carl or Carrie.

Inching his way along the rock face, he spotted Brady coming from the other side. Matt held a finger to his lips and then pointed toward the solid mass of rock to his left. Brady's eyes widened. He took a step closer. Matt did too. Suddenly the opening appeared before him, and Matt shrank back. A cry rent the quivering morning air and a shot rang out, followed by a scream.

Before Matt and Brady could rush into the crevice in the rock, Carl Cheatham stumbled from the narrow cave opening and tumbled down to the layer of rock below. Then he took off running back to his camp and his horses without so much as a backward glance. Matt slung the rifle round and took aim, a red furious rage burning in his belly, but Brady darted forward and lowered the barrel with one hand, his gaze fixed on Matt's eyes.

"Never shoot a man in the back," he said flatly. "That's the surest way to kill two men with one bullet."

Matt swallowed and felt the red haze fade from his sight. He nodded and looked down. "Thanks, Brady," he said, knowing they both understood the deeper meaning of what had just happened.

"Brady? Matt?" Carrie's shaky voice reached their ears, and they both rushed to her side where she stood in the crevice, leaning shakily against the rock wall. Brady took his sister in his arms in a brotherly embrace.

"Shhhh... You're safe, Sis. Hush now, hush..." he crooned softly, sounding more fatherly that Matt had ever heard him. Matt shoved his hands in his pockets, unsure what to do with himself in that tender moment. It seemed selfish to wish that Carrie was in his arms, but he couldn't stop the thought from running through his mind. He vehemently reminded himself the most important thing was that she was safe and Carl Cheatham was unlikely to bother them anymore.

With his back to the rock face and his friends, Matt stared out over the wide expanse of prairie rolling away into the distance. It felt like he could see clearly to the end of the world. Far below, a winding creek meandered its way along the valley floor and a flock of water birds rose into the air in a gaggling cloud of shining feathers, drowning out the rapid but faint hoofbeats that told him of Carl Cheatham's escape.

He could hear Brady and Carrie talking behind him, but he purposely didn't listen to what they were saying. He was struggling with the awful feeling in his gut that he might just have killed a man. Nobody had warned him it was a possibility out in the Wild West. It had been the furthest thing from his mind. All he had wanted was to see the beautiful new land his father had shown them in the brochures he had brought into their safe and uneventful lives.

The worst part of it was that he knew, given the choice to do it over, he would not hesitate to shoot again. A sense of fear and awe settled on him. He had, in a split second, made the choice between who should live and who should die. If he had not pulled the trigger, chances were good that Max would be alive and Brady would be dead. But who was he to make that choice? His mother had often reminded them that revenge was the Lord's and that all men's times were in His hands.

Matt unclenched his fists and looked down at his shaking fingers. A soft, cool hand lighted on his shoulder and he turned to look into Carrie's red-rimmed but deeply grateful olive green eyes.

"Brady told me what you did, Matt," she whispered. "Thank you."

Matt looked at her long and hard. All he could do was nod and try to swallow down the painful lump in his throat. He could feel tears welling in his eyes and felt helpless to hold them back.

"It's not your fault, you hear?" she whispered, her own eyes tearing up again. "He left you no choice. You did the right thing, Matt."

Matt wanted desperately to believe her. He had to hope that, one day, he would.

Chapter 13
Unexpected Providence

Clyde peered into the haziness of the midmorning light. The prairie grasses and sweet sage shimmered in the sun that was already piercing through the fabric of his shirt and burning his skin. The trail ahead showed no sign of his son or of Brady or Carrie.

"They'll be all right," Anna said beside him as she hooked her arm into his. "You'll see. I've been praying ever since they took off into the night, and I have peace in my soul. They'll be back, don't you fret, love."

Clyde felt his gut twist, and he glanced at Landon walking up ahead, his eyes fixed on the horizon, scanning it left and right with clockwork regularity. Then he looked down at Anna and placed an arm around her shoulders. "If that's what you believe, then that's what I believe, too," he said, wishing he sounded more convincing, but Anna didn't seem to notice. She slipped her arm around his waist and squeezed.

"Pa, we're tired. Can we stop and rest a bit soon? Can we?" Billy's voice turned Clyde's attention from his wife and fully onto the little boy beside him. His son's face seemed thinner than he could remember seeing it before, and Tess, who walked beside her brother, wasn't filling out her dress the way she used to. Losing their horse was clearly taking its toll on his two youngest children.

Clyde tousled the little boy's hair. "I know, buddy. So am I, but we've got to keep going. We don't want to make Matt and Brady wait too long before we find them and Carrie."

"They're going to be even more tired than we are," Nellie added, joining the rest of her family and taking Tess's hand as she fell in step with them. "They'll need us to be strong for them. Especially you, Billy-boy."

"Clyde! I see something!" Landon cut in on any response Billy might have made. He was looking back at them from the rise ahead and waving his hands in the air. "Grab your rifle!"

Clyde didn't hesitate for a moment. Reaching into the front of the wagon, he hauled out the weapon Landon had referred to and jogged up to the front of the train. Sure enough, up ahead a horse and rider and two people on foot beside them came plodding over the rise. The sun was full in their faces, so they kept them shielded from the glare, but Clyde and Landon could clearly see it was their beloved children, returning to them alive.

All fatigue faded into obscurity as Clyde took off running. Tears streamed down his cheeks unchecked at the sight of Matt stumbling along, his shirt torn and grubby, his rifle still slung across his back, his hand gripping the reins of a shaggy painted pony on which Carrie sat. His lungs burned and his legs ached, but he did not stop until he had enveloped his son in an ecstatic, breathless embrace.

Words seemed superfluous when he drew back and looked into the eyes of his boy who was a boy no more. He simply smiled, feeling sad and yet in awe as he vigorously rubbed Matt's upper arm, wanting to somehow convey to him how proud he also felt in that moment. Brady's voice broke in on father and son's silent communication.

"Our Matt proved himself a good man with a rifle today, Mr. Henderson," he stated with genuine admiration in his tone.

Matt shook his head. "I killed a man," he corrected his friend hoarsely.

"He killed an evil man who was about to kill my brother." Carrie's voice carried down from the horse she still sat on, her white nightdress partly covered by Matt's dark blue coat.

"Sometimes good men need t' do bad things to stop bad men doin' worse things," Landon stated, his voice deep with unspoken emotion. Clyde saw him lock eyes with Matt, and he knew they were communicating in a language he had not yet learned. He wished he could have walked that territory before his son, yet he felt grateful Landon was there to guide him through the unwanted but unavoidable experience.

The returning heroes and the shaken but unharmed Carrie were hustled back to the wagons, which were quickly drawn into a circle formation for an early nooning since it was barely eleven o'clock. Clyde stared out at the two small bumps on the horizon while he ate his meal. Brady had pointed them out as the place where he and Matt had finally launched an attack on the kidnappers and rescued Carrie.

"I'm hopin' by sundown we'll roll on by Courthouse Rock," Landon remarked, as if reading Clyde's mind.

"And after that is Chimney Rock, isn't it, Mr. Morland?" Billy piped up, his fatigue only slightly staved off by the prospect of reaching the much bespoken milestone.

"It sure is, half-pint," Landon agreed, chewing and swallowing a piece of pan bread before he continued. "That should take us another day and a half, two days. Then we'll still have a good seventy-five miles of pretty rough country before we reach Laramie."

Clyde watched Landon. His demeanor had been mostly confident and calm, and sometimes a little urgent, impatient even. Since Carrie's kidnapping, he had become exponentially more watchful and visibly fidgety. He didn't seem to hear the complaints of the worn-out travelers with him. His eyes and ears were far more watchful toward what was going on beyond the huddle of wagons.

Clyde knew what was haunting his compatriot. He feared the same thing: the return of Carl Cheatham. He had not seemed like someone who gave up easily. That night, as they camped beyond the looming buttresses of the Courthouse and Jailhouse Rocks, Landon made sure all the womenfolk were surrounded by men with rifles. The remaining animals were kept inside the circle, and they relieved the guard at shorter intervals to make sure whoever was on duty was wide awake.

As soon as they were on their weary way again the next morning, Clyde fell in step beside Landon as he strode ahead of the wagons to scout the trail. "Seventy-five miles after Chimney Rock. That far, eh?" he asked. He didn't think it necessary to elaborate on the reason for his query.

"Uh-huh," Landon confirmed, not taking his eyes from their sweeping surveillance of the hills and dales around them.

"You think he'll come back before we reach the fort?" Clyde prodded further.

"It ain't impossible is all I'm sayin'. Chances that he'll take revenge are slim, but I'll wager he ain't given up on gettin' what he wants, and the only way he's gettin' what he wants is over my dead body."

"There isn't another way around?" Clyde asked, grasping at straws. "Maybe if we take a different route, we can shake him off."

"Not that I know of. Folks say Scott's Bluff ain't passable for wagons. Unless we want t' risk breaking a few axles, that ain't a good choice."

Clyde fell to silence, and they both stared ahead at the looming, almost unnaturally narrow finger of rock that pointed upward to the hazy sky. For many emigrants before them, it had stood as a silent confirmation that they were still on track. Clyde wondered how many would pass that way and feel encouraged, as he did, by its towering spire.

He knew what Anna would say. *It's a reminder from our almighty Father God that we should look up, to Him, for strength, courage, and wisdom for the rest of our journey.* He could almost hear her voice in his head. Then Landon's finger pointing into the distance caught his eye.

"We'll roll on by the left and camp out there beyond the rock tonight," he said matter-of-factly.

"Sounds good to me," Clyde agreed, and left him standing astride a deep gouge in the earth that could only have been carved out by the passage of many iron-clad wagon wheels. He made his way back to the slowly moving wagons and walked along the length of them.

"We'll camp on the other side of Chimney Rock tonight," he announced to each family as they passed him. Some merely nodded, too tired to respond. Others made polite conversation. Some asked details about when they could expect to reach Fort Laramie. It had become as much a point of interest to the adults as Chimney Rock had been to the children.

When he reached the Southeys' wagon, the pale, emaciated look of all of them arrested Clyde's attention. "Are you folks all right?" he asked with concern. "You look rather poorly to me."

"We've been gettin' the backdoor trots for a few days now, Mr. Henderson," Ned Southey confessed in a whisper. "We were hopin' it would sort itself out, but, well, let's just say it's been a downhill path."

"Dysentery?" Clyde queried, wanting to make sure he had understood the man's rather ham-fisted euphemism correctly.

"That's the one," Tilly Southey, Ned's wife, replied grimly. "Greg Sawyer's got it, too. Henry Baker and his lot been makin' a lot of trips to the bushes lately. And I won't be surprised if Arthur Riley's lot are comin' down with it, you mark my words." The sweat beaded her forehead as she spoke, and she wiped it away with an already nearly soaked handkerchief that looked like it might once have been white.

Clyde wondered why nobody had spoken up sooner. He hurried along the rest of the wagon train, adding to his repeated repertoire the question of each group's health. The results were less than heartening.

"Dysentery?" Landon echoed after Clyde had reported back to him on his findings.

"Looks that way."

Landon groaned and stomped back along the line of wagons that Clyde had just come from. Clyde himself turned to look at the clouds already gathering on the western horizon, and knew they would be lucky to make it past their chosen landmark before nightfall. He was right, and when the wagons had circled for the night with Chimney Rock just to the east of them and the children were busy with their chores, he drew the wagon train leader aside.

"This means we'll be even later to Laramie, doesn't it?" He already knew the answer.

"Darn right it does, barrin' a miracle," Landon growled. "Some of 'em been fallin' farther and farther behind each day. I was wonderin' why. Well, now I know. Worst of it is we can't load 'em sick folk in the wagons, those oxen are already plumb wore out from the heat and the terrain." He pushed his hat back on his head and scratched his scalp just above the hairline, looking as close to exasperated as Matt had ever seen him.

"I believe in miracles, Landon," Anna's voice broke in on their conversation. She was fetching something in the wagon and had clearly overheard their conversation. "In fact, I've been praying to the good Lord to send us one."

"Well, ma'am," Landon bobbed his head in a show of respect, "I sure hope He hears ya."

They had scarcely cleared away the supper dishes when the wind howled and the first hailstones fell, bouncing along on the trampled grass inside the circle of wagons. The screams of women and children filled the air, at first excited and then more frantic as the orbs of ice pelted down on them with ferocious force. Soon their voices were all but drowned out by the booming, echoing thunder that followed wild streaks of lightning, flashing close upon each other's heels.

Clyde huddled in the wagon with his family, holding a tearful Tess in his lap and listening to the storm belting out all its fury beyond the canvas cover. Landon had suggested they line the inside with more layers of cloth, anything they could find, and they had done just that. It did not stop the driving rain from seeping through and dripping down onto them in disconsolate little drops. But he hoped it would prevent the hailstones from tearing the canvas to shreds, as Landon had intimated.

In the morning, the wisdom of his words was clear. Those who had not heeded Landon's advice now had coverings flapping on their wagons that looked more like lace curtains than waterproofed canvas coverings. Some had the bruises to prove the stones had reached the size of chicken eggs at the height of the storm's fury. To top it all off, three of the families—the Southeys, Rileys, and Bakers—were mostly too weak to travel, their dysentery having ravaged their bodies to mere shadows of their former selves.

Clyde stared up at the reaching finger of Chimney Rock. *God, are you hearing my wife's prayers?* he asked, not really expecting an answer himself but sensing there was a longing in his spirit for someone to hear and respond to his helpless soul cry.

As he turned away, his eye traveled down to the base of the rock formation, and he instantly froze. A lone horseman stood silhouetted against a sky full of the misty gray, scudding remnants of ragged clouds left over from the previous night's storm. For a moment he thought it was Carl, then he noticed the unmistakable outline of two large feathers waving gently above the rider's head in the morning breeze.

"A Sioux," Connor's voice said beside him, making him jump. "Who knows how many more of them are waiting just over that rise, and us a flock of sittin' ducks, ready to pluck and boil." He lifted his rifle to his shoulder.

Clyde reached out and forced it down before Connor could even take aim. He fought down the irritation that made him want to lash out angrily at the young man. "Have you already forgotten what Landon told us the time we met up with the Pawnees?" he reminded Connor, not taking his eyes off the stationary man on his horse.

"Hold your fire until they shoot first," Connor replied, his voice grating with agitation. He was clearly spoiling for a fight.

"Shooting folks isn't the best way to deal with boredom," Clyde quipped, but his voice faded away on the last two syllables. The man was motioning to them in what appeared to be some kind of sign language. Clyde held up his hand and then shrugged his shoulders in a gesture of not understanding. "Hey, Landon!" Connor called out. "You know any sign language?"

Landon was by their side in a flash, his eyes riveted on the silhouette against the horizon. The man repeated the gestures. "He says he's friendly. A medicine man," Landon said, sounding slightly mystified. "Says he wants to talk."

"I think we should let him," Anna said, joining the three menfolk, along with most of the other family members gawking at the impressive sight.

"How romantic," Nellie sighed as they watched the rider descend the slopes of Chimney Rock and make his way toward the emigrant camp.

"Clyde, you and me'll go out to meet him. Show of good faith if we meet him on neutral ground," Landon said crisply, his eyes shrewdly darting from the approaching stranger to the slopes of Chimney Rock, then to the surrounding countryside. "Connor, you let everyone know there's to be no crowdin' nor starin', and especially no shootin' unless a hostile shoots first. You hear?"

"Aye-aye, sir!" Connor replied, tongue-in-cheek, and bounded away to complete the task given him.

Clyde followed Landon out beyond the protection of the circled wagons and straight toward the stranger.

"Looks like Oglala Sioux," Landon remarked almost to himself as they came closer, and more details of their unexpected visitor's appearance became visible. "An old man. That's good. They're usually wiser, less fire and froth than the young warriors."

When they had come within a few yards of each other, the man raised his hand and reined in his sorrel horse. He slid down to the ground with a grace and ease that Clyde could not remember seeing in a horseman before. Landon stopped, holding out one hand in front of Clyde's chest, so he stopped too. The man sat down cross-legged on the wet ground. Landon followed suit, grabbing Clyde by the shirtsleeve and pulling him down beside him.

Clyde watched in awe as the man signed, and Landon signed back in response. He did not know what they were talking about, so he contented himself with taking in the details of the man's outfit. He had on the same fringed, decorated buckskin pants as the Sioux who had clearly worked for Carl.

His chest was bare, except for an almost scarf-like necklace made entirely of small beads woven into a simple striped pattern of blue and white. Another necklace, consisting of many long strands of multicolored beads, looped across the first one. Across his shoulders hung a garment like a stole made of what appeared to be brown bear fur decorated with doubloons dotted in a widely spaced line down the middle.

Brass armbands glinted on his upper arms, and from his ears hung two small white shells. His head was covered with a beaver hat Clyde guessed must have been acquired from a fur trapper. Behind it, the man's long, flowing black locks cascaded freely down his back. Atop the hat, a mess of feathers from many birds formed a strange nest, crowned by the two white tipped eagle feathers.

His skin was leathery and dark, but what captured Clyde's attention most were his eyes. They were deep brown to the point of being black, but there was a look in them that stirred something of awe in Clyde and gave him a comforting sense of being safe.

"He says he knows we're havin' a hard time of it." Landon's voice broke in on Clyde's examination of the stranger. It was filled with the same awe Clyde was feeling. Neither of them took their eyes off their visitor when Landon added quietly. "He says the Great Spirit sent him to help us."

Chapter 14
Answered Prayers

After much signing and careful translation by Landon, the medicine man's story was made clear. His name was Black Fox, and he had dreamed of the long finger of rock pointing to the sky. In the dream, the bald eagle had flown over the rock and then the shadow of its outstretched wings had fallen on the little circle of wagons just beyond the base of the landmark. He had been gathering field herbs a few miles away and had ridden across during the night.

Landon spoke in staccato syllables while he signed. "You… can… treat… bad… stomach?"

Black Fox nodded and shook a leather bag at his side. Clyde could hear the rattling of dry leaves and sticks inside. He said a few syllables that Clyde could not decipher and signed again.

"He wants us to make a tea with the herbs in his bag and make them drink a *lot*," Logan translated thoughtfully. "It sounds like he's talking about sunflower heads. And he says the healthy men must hunt buffalo and the women make bone broth. Lots of that, too. Thank… you… wise… medicine… man…" Landon spoke out his hand signals as he signed. "Louise, help our guest with fire and a pot. Brady, is there still fresh drinking water? Round up the healthy fellers and fetch us enough from the river. Take the painted pony. Clyde, you and me are goin' t' shoot us a couple of buffalo."

The settlers, who had been staring, some of them open-mouthed, at the medicine man who had accompanied their leaders into the midst of their camp, now sprang into action. A flurry of activity followed as the affected individuals were prepped to receive their doses of medicine as soon as it was ready. Brady commandeered Matt and three other young men who were sharing a wagon, and they took off with every bucket, waterskin, and canteen they could lay their hands on.

Clyde fetched his rifle from the wagon and then stopped as he came face to face with Landon. "We don't have any horses," they said in unison. Clyde's heart dropped into his boots.

Landon turned and signed to Black Fox. Some more signing followed that had Clyde's head turning from the one to the other and back again, although he could not make out head or tail of what they were communicating.

"He'll drive some over the ridge for us so we can shoot 'em down from inside the ravine near the rock," Landon condensed the discussion. The medicine man was already riding off on his horse to herd the ill-fated buffalo. Clyde and Landon gave each other one look and set off for the famous landmark at a jog.

Three times a day for two days, Black Fox cooked tea from sunflower heads and some other herbs and roots he added to the brew. The sick emigrants grimaced as they drank it down, but there was a marked improvement in their condition, and by the end of the second day, they were looking perkier than they had before they became sick. That evening, Black Fox sat with them round the campfire instead of disappearing into the dark as he had every other night before that.

He signed something and Landon translated. "He wants to know where we're going next."

At Landon's signed response, Black Fox signed again.

"He says he can show us a shorter way, but we ain't allowed to tell another soul about it," Landon translated.

Clyde was about to ask if Landon thought they could trust him when the shrewd but benign eyes in the medicine man's wrinkled face caught his attention. For two days he had stayed close and boiled tea for sick strangers. He had chanted his haunting, melancholy chants and shaken a dry, hollowed-out gourd filled with seed over the writhing forms of groaning invalids.

Nobody had told him to do that. *Except the Great Spirit,* Clyde thought to himself, remembering Black Fox's own telling of why he had ridden over to Chimney Rock when his intended path would have taken him an entirely different way. He wondered if this was God's interesting way of answering Anna's prayers.

In the morning, Black Fox was there, silently leading the way, the caravan of tattered wagons following him in solemn procession along the trail. They made good time. To Clyde, it felt as if their self-appointed guide's presence going before them excited a fresh energy in the travelers. Even his own steps felt as if they had a little more spring in them.

They traveled close along the North Platte for the first day, and then on the morning of the second day, they left the shimmering expanse of waters behind, staying on a solidly western trajectory while the broad, shallow mass of water turned away from them, coming more from the north than the west. Ahead, shimmering in the distance, were the ridges and crags of Scott's Bluff.

Black Fox led them almost to the great gateway that seemed to have been carved out of the rock by some massive hand, and they stopped for noon. Black Fox motioned to Landon to meet him outside of the wagon circle. The two men spoke in sign language for a few minutes, and then Black Fox turned his horse's head in the butte's direction to the right of the gate.

Landon stood watching him ride away for a while, then he turned and strolled back to the camp. He was silent for the rest of the meal and seemed more anxious than usual for his emigrant party to get back on the trail again. When they did, he led the way, glancing up now and then at the butte that Black Fox had ridden toward.

As the lead wagon pitched and rolled cumbersomely over the uneven ground, Clyde wondered if their guide had led them to a more treacherous path that would cost them in effort what they might gain in distance. He was about to share this thought with Landon, looking up from the wagon he was helping maneuver around a large ditch, when he stopped and stepped aside, his mouth agape.

Soldiers were dotted about the pass, among them Oglala Sioux. They were digging away and leveling off ridges, carting rocks from one place to another and stamping them down, and filling the long lines of ditches that ran along the bottom of the pass with sand. Beyond them, a ribbon of dark earth ran off into the distance, looking for all the world like one of the main streets in Philadelphia, minus the buildings, carriages, and people.

Clyde laughed as Anna came up alongside him to see what he was staring at. "Ah," she said, a smile in her voice. "He will make a way in the wilderness. I just read that from our Bible this morning, if you remember."

"I do remember," Clyde replied, shaking his head in wonderment.

As the line of wagons made their way up onto the crude and incomplete road, one of the soldiers raised his hat to them. "Reckon you're the first to use our new road, then. Never figured it would get used so fast. We ain't even done," he remarked with a grin.

"We had a special escort," Landon replied. "Don't reckon you'll see too many more of us before you are done." He glanced up at the butte to the right of the pass. Clyde followed his gaze. Just as he had appeared on the slopes of Chimney Rock, Black Fox now sat his horse on the slopes below the sandstone peak of the butte.

"Look, Pa!" Billy exclaimed excitedly, pointing at the mass of yellowish rock. "That butte looks like an eagle!"

Clyde had to admit he was right. A great eagle made of rock hovered above them with his wings spread wide protectively over the gaping pass between the line of rock outcroppings.

"If you screw up your eyes a little, he looks like he's lookin' to the west," Billy added, wrinkling up his nose and his eyes.

"So he does, so he does," Clyde agreed, smiling.

"You folks just follow this road, beyond that's a track that'll take y'all right up t' the fort," the friendly cavalryman informed them.

"Can't say we expected this," Landon replied gratefully. "But we sure ain't complaining."

After the weeks of arduous trudging through the heat, navigating around dips and ditches and ridges in the earth, even the unfinished, crude roadway ahead seemed like a highway to heaven to the weary travelers. It indeed led to a trail that was easy to follow and met up once more with the ever narrowing North Platte river.

After three days of almost dreamy travel, the sprawling settlement came into view beyond the gurgling waters of a shallow creek that fed into the Platte. Stately two-story buildings stood beside long rows of barracks. Checkered blocks of nearly white tents stood in evenly spaced lines. Wagons and oxen and people of all descriptions crowded the surrounding hills.

"It's like a city!" Nellie declared.

"Hardly," Helen countered. "Though I dare say it is nice to see at least some semblance of civilization again." Her words lacked the usual edge to them, and she sounded almost pleasant.

"What's going on over there?" Billy wondered out loud, pointing toward a mob, yelling and waving their fists in the air near a plantation of small trees. As the train drew closer, the cheering and jeering rose to a crescendo and then slowly died away. The crowd dispersed, some hoarse oaths still erupting now and then in anger.

"Better turn your eyes the other way, gals," Brady said suddenly. "Looks like a lynchin' to me, don't you think, Pa?"

Landon nodded. "Sure does," he agreed.

"Land sakes!" Connor cried after they had gone a few more yards. "It's Carl and Amos!"

Even the women couldn't avert their eyes anymore after hearing that, though the mothers hid their little girls' faces in their skirts. Clyde and Landon looked over to the lynching tree. Sure enough, the two horse thieves cum kidnappers each dangled lifelessly at the end of a rope.

"Well, what do you know," Landon remarked grimly. "Looks like their thievin' caught up with them before we did."

"You know those varmints, mister?" a passing soldier asked, apparently hearing the men talk.

"We sure do. Though I reckon we won't miss 'em too much. Stole some horses and other valuables from us back near Courthouse Rock," Landon replied.

"Well, now, that figures," the soldier chuckled. "Both of 'em were caught stealin' horses this mornin', though hell knows why. They already had themselves a string of fine animals. I reckon if you could describe your missin' horses to the general, why, he'd be happy t' pass 'em on to their rightful owners."

Clyde gripped Anna's hand. "You don't stop praying to God, you hear, love?" he whispered.

Anna squeezed his fingers. "Next time, why don't you join me?"

Clyde grunted. He wasn't ready. Not yet. But there was one thing he could say that didn't need a reply. *Thank You, God.*

"You know what day it is today, right, Clyde?" Landon's voice interrupted his short, heartfelt prayer of gratitude.

Clyde looked up in slight confusion. "Thursday?" he postulated uncertainly.

"Darn right. It's Thursday, July fourth. We made it bang on time!"

Clyde followed Landon's pointing finger. Bonfires were being set up, much bigger than the usual campfires, and here and there the fizz, pop, and bang of a firework going off could already be heard.

"Well, we better circle the wagons and set up camp so we don't miss out on any of the fun, especially considering we've got so much to celebrate." Clyde laughed.

Landon joined in with his deep-throated chuckle. "And what better way than with an Independence Day celebration?"

"On the road to independence," Billy piped up.

Clyde reached out and ruffled his son's hair. "Exactly right, Billy. Exactly right. And just as it did in 1776, independence is going to cost us something. Probably a lot of something."

"I don't know about you, folks," Landon said with a nod, "but it's a price I'm willin' t' pay."

The End

I hope you enjoyed this story.

I would appreciate a positive review on Amazon

Watch for more Classic Westerns...coming soon.